# Great Uncle Sedgwick's Gift

## Part 3

**By Beth E Browning**

## Acknowledgements

My many thanks to my young friends, Lewis Norris and Alicia Munday for their critiques.
Also my thanks to Sandy, Melva, Sue, Moyra, Kim, Wendy and other friends and writers from Brampton Road Adult Institute for their encouragement.

E mail  Bethbrowning1@hotmail.com
Website - bethbrowning-writer.com

Trunks- Cynoclub /dreamtime
Clip Art/ balloon-sweep
ISBN 978- 1-326-17867-3

## Introduction

### Wattle Peak

It was an early spring day in 1980 as Sedgwick Pendleton slowly made his way to the cliff's edge, outside his properties at Wattle Peak. He had lived there for all of his 86 years, his once blonde hair now completely white.

Sedgwick leant on the iron railings, and peered down the stairway cut into the 50 foot high craggy granite cliff. This was the only way to reach the creek and the sandy bay below, other than at low tide.

To his left was the waterfall, in full flow after the winter rains. It's waters came from the stream that ran alongside his garden and the old farmhouse before pouring spectacularly over the cliff's edge, crashing onto the rocks below. The waters flowed on into the creek near the small jetty and finally made their way to the sea.

Sedgwick turned and proudly viewed the old farmhouse, which formed part of the front boundary of his land. It was very old, built in 1580 of wattle and daub; a rough wooden framed construction covered with plaster and clay mixed with straw. Over the centuries it had been altered and repaired many times. Behind it, to the left, set back from the road stood, the red bricked Georgian House. All that now remained of the farmland was a large garden.

He had always loved these old houses and was sure the next generation would love them too. The houses were only twenty minutes away from the oldest parts of the nearest town, Pennington, when using the footpaths. The town had two schools. It was a good place to live and bring up children. Sedgwick had no children of his own. His affairs were all in order, and Sedgwick made his way to the farmhouse and slowly climbed the back stairs into the attic. There was a letter in his hand ready to put in a secret place, where he knew it would be found in the near future. He smiled, imagining the astonished looks on the faces of his nephew Henry's children when they read it. How he envied them their adventures to come.

Shortly after Great Uncle Sedgwick died the Robertson family moved into the Georgian house he had left to them. The old farmhouse, too, had been bequeathed to them and its attic given solely to the three children, along with the three very special trunks found therein. As explained in the letter found at the bottom of the oldest trunk, these trunks would enable Beth, her twin brother Mike and younger brother Jake to travel back in time to three eras. They were only fifteen visits to each era in turn over a three year period ending New Year's Eve. Each trunk contained clothes, money and artifacts of that era. Once they had donned the clothes and placed their own clothes in the trunk and, most importantly closed the lid the room would whirl and the air sparkle as they began each of their adventures.

---

## Chapter 1

### And Then There Were Four

The whirling stopped and the sparkles ceased as they arrived back from their final visit to the Georgian era. It was icy cold and New Year's Eve, of the year 1981. Quickly they took their clothes out of the second of the three trunks and changed out of their Georgian costumes, putting on their own everyday clothes, shivering as they did so in the freezing farmhouse attic. Jake the youngest, at twelve years old, was first down the stairs and out of the tack room door, hurrying home slightly ahead of his thirteen and half years old brother and sister, twins Beth and Mike. They had just finished their amazing 15 visits to the year 1760, in the Georgian era, made possible by the very special gift left them by their late Great Uncle Sedgwick.

Beth felt very sad having just said goodbye there to their Great Uncle James, who they had met for the very first time and quite unexpectedly in 1760. James had willingly remained in the Georgian era, in the year 1755, after having arrived there from the year 1908, with Great Uncle Sedgwick and Great Aunt Anna, his brother and sister, on their journeys to the past. Beth and her brothers now knew why James hadn't died in 1908, as stated on the plaque in the church.

There was now only one era left for them to visit, the Victorian era, having already visited both Cromwell's time and the Georgian period. Their adventures in those periods, Beth knew, none of them would ever forget.

Beth, Mike and Jake now had with them an unexpected guest from 1760, Sooty, a small cute cocker spaniel, with a slightly curly glossy black coat. Sooty ran alongside them, his tail wagging madly, giving the occasional excited bark.

They had thought of leaving Sooty overnight, nearby in the farmhouse attic, safely out of sight of their parents. However, they just couldn't bear to leave him on his own and knew it could be very cold in there. It would be too dangerous to leave him alone, with the electric fire on.

"Quiet," whispered Mike to Sooty, as they made their way up the drive to the front door. Mike picked up Sooty and hid him inside his coat before Beth opened the door cautiously, and peeked in. Beth was pleased that their parents were nowhere in sight. All four made their way stealthily up the stairs to Mike's bedroom.

"He will need a bed," said Beth, scratching the dog behind his ears and in return he gave her hand a grateful lick.

"He could sleep on my bed," replied Mike, eagerly.

"I doubt mum would approve of that and we need to start off right, by keeping in her good books. After all, we won't be able to keep Sooty a secret forever," commented Beth, giving Sooty a loving look.

“We could make a temporary bed out of one of those old blankets that we held onto in our attic,” suggested Jake with a grin.

“That’s not a bad idea,” said Mike, “I’ll go and get one, while you two keep watch,” and off he dashed.

Mike had placed the folded blanket on the far side of his bed and went and stood in the doorway checking that it couldn’t be seen from there. As they watched, Sooty curled upon it, yawned and settled down to a snooze. Beth was pleased it was to the little dog’s liking.

They heard their mother call up the stairs, “Dinner is ready and it’s snowing.” On looking out into the dark night, they were disappointed to see a light dusting of snow and thought of the fun they would have if it got heavier and settled. So as not to disturb Sooty, they quietly closed the door and headed down to their large and warm kitchen, where mum was busy putting their dinner plates on the table. It was their favourite dish, sausages, mash and baked beans mixed with tinned Italian plum tomatoes sweetened with a little sugar.

“What have you been up to today? I didn’t hear you all come in,” their mother remarked, as she settled down to join them, after having placed an extra dinner on the worktop for their father who would be home later.

“We have been visiting friends. I don’t think we will see them again,” replied Beth sadly. “On Boxing Day, they lost their eldest daughter Lucinda, only eighteen, after a short illness and decided to return home to Leeds rather than stay until her father's work contract finished. They said it was too painful to remain here where they had seen her so happy. Her younger sister is the same age as Mike and me. Mike had been helping to train her sister's dog, Sooty, a lovely little black spaniel and Mike has even taught it to do tricks. We shall miss them all."

"I expect you will," said her mother, as she patted Beth's hand sympathetically. "So that's why you have all been so quiet today and why I found what looked like dog biscuits in Mike's jeans pocket when I was preparing them ready for the wash. What a sad thing to happen and it's not a good time for your friends to be travelling so far, with possible ice and snow on the roads.

"Now will you be alright on your own this evening, while your father and I go to the William's for their New Year's party, we'll only be down the road?"

"Oh mum, you needn't worry about us, after all, Mike and I will be fourteen soon," said Beth, confidently.

"Well, you will be in May. Why is it children are in such a hurry to grow up," she muttered, as she pushed her chair under the table. "Alright, but the phone number is on the sideboard, if you should need us."

"I've left out some sweets and crisps for you and there's lemonade and other treats in the fridge. As it's New Year you can stay up until to midnight, if you wish, but then it's straight to bed."

"Sure," replied Mike and the others nodded. While this conversation had been going on, Jake had hidden half a sausage in his paper napkin and Beth had done the same.

They all helped clear the table, while mum prepared the custard for their apple pie. Their mother looked surprised when they offered to do the washing up.

Furtively, they took it in turns to check on Sooty, taking up a water bowl and a dish filled with the cut up sausage, much to the little dog's delight.

At 9 pm their parents left for the Williams' house and as soon as they were out of sight, Mike brought Sooty downstairs to enjoy the evening by the fire, while they watched the TV in the sitting room.

A little later Beth returned from the kitchen. "We really need to get some dog food," she said, "we've got spaghetti bolognaise tomorrow night and I don't think we can smuggle that out in a paper napkin. How many dog biscuits do you have left, Mike?"

"Only a few, so they won't last long."

"Well," said Beth, "I've cut up some cheese into small pieces and placed them in a small plastic box but it's not good for Sooty to have too much of that. It's a pity the shops will be closed tomorrow as its New Year's Day." Disappearing back into the kitchen once more, she added a tin of corned beef, cut into small cubes, to the plastic box before returning to the sitting room.

"Keep the box on the sill outside your window Mike, as it's so cold it shouldn't go off. Remind me to buy a replacement tin when we do get to the shops."

Mike, concerned that Sooty might make a mess in the house, took him out for a quick walk around the garden, hurrying back inside to the fire to warm himself up once more. Jake had found a small ball and bounced it to see how high Sooty could jump. Excitedly, Sooty jumped high into the air but the ball bounced awkwardly, causing a vase to fall off the table and smash.

"Oh no," cried Jake, "that wasn't supposed to happen."

"You wally! We were trying to keep in mum's good books, remember," said Beth exasperated.

"I'm sorry," said Jake, "do you think she'll notice?"

"Maybe not for a few days," replied Mike, giving his brother a nudge. "We will have to see if we can find another like it in town. Put one from the kitchen there for now, there are a few under the sink."

He replaced the broken vase with one of a similar shape and placed the bits of broken china in the outside bin along with the empty corned beef tin.

A little before midnight, Beth stood up and yawned, "Time for bed," she said and headed upstairs to get ready, "mum and dad will be back soon."

Once ready, all three crowded around the window in their parents' bedroom. It had the best view and as they looked out into the dark night, watching the fireworks, they heard midnight strike on the local church clock, on a clear frosty night. "There's still only a thin covering of snow, not enough for even a proper snowball fight or to enjoy our sledges on the hill. What a pity," said Mike, as the last of the fireworks died away.

"Yeah, but further snow has been forecast in a few days' time," said Jake with glee.

"Look how the frost sparkles in the moonlight," said Beth. They stood admiring the sight until Mike yawned setting them all off.

"Oh, goodnight," said Mike, yawning, and headed off to bed with Sooty by his side. The other two soon followed

***

The next morning, Sooty crept onto Mike's bed and licked his face, until he woke up. "Okay, okay," he said, "I suppose you want to go out." Half asleep, Mike wandered down into the hall and struggled to put on his wellies. Still in his pyjamas and dressing gown, Mike took Sooty into the garden where he did his business in a flower bed. Shivering, they hurried back inside. Being still very early they happily returned to bed. When Beth peered in later both Mike and Sooty were curled up together on the bed and fast asleep.

***

# 12

Once the shops reopened they managed to buy several cans of dog food, a tin of corned beef and a vase. During the four days Sooty had been with them, a routine had been worked out to ensure he wasn't seen. On the fifth day when it got dark, they crept into the house and were settling Sooty into Mike's room when they heard their mother call out, "Beth, Mike, Jake, may I see you in the sitting room, please." When they entered the room, they noticed their father was also there, sitting by the fire in his new dark blue jumper that mum had bought him for Christmas.

"Do you have something you'd like to tell us?" said their father, with one eyebrow raised.

"Maybe," replied Beth, unsure as to what her father was referring.

"Only maybe?" asked their mother.

"Well, we did not think you would notice," said Mike, "we did replace it with one very similar."

"You did?" queried their mother with a quizzical look. 'Drats,' thought Beth –'he had obviously guessed wrong'.

"We broke a vase but we bought another," said Beth.

"Oh," said her mother, "I knew something was different in here but couldn't quite put my finger on it." She walked over and examined the vase. "I must say the one you bought is a pretty good replacement. Luckily the original wasn't valuable."

Before she could turn around, the three children went to make a quick exit as their father called out, “Not so fast there. Are you sure you have nothing else to tell us?”

“What about?” queried Mike, learning by his earlier mistake.

“Well, unless you’ve taken to eating dog food I assume there must be another explanation for the tins in the bin,” said their Mother.

“I don’t suppose you would accept we could be feeding the badgers,” said Jake, shrugging his shoulders.

“Good try Jake, but the dog tracks in the frost tell another story,” said their father, with a grin.

All three children started to talk at once about it being a lovely dog, no trouble, that it would be an asset, as it would deter burglars. “Whoa,” shouted their father, hardly able to make out what each had said. “Mike, go and fetch the dog from wherever you have been hiding it.”

“Oh, mum, dad, PLEASE say we can keep it,” pleaded Beth, near to tears, as Mike entered the room with Sooty by his side.

“Here Sooty,” called Mary and the dog came to her tail, wagging wildly, as he tried to get on to her lap. Mary laughed, stroked the dog and tickled him under his chin.

“How did you know it was Sooty?” asked Jake.

“Well, it all fitted,” said their Father, “after your mother told me about your friends leaving.”

“Please can we keep him,” said Mike, “they have moved away now and we promised them to find Sooty a good home but honestly he would be no trouble.”

Their parents looked at each other and at Sooty, before smiling, as their father replied, “Yes, why not.” The children were all over their parents with Sooty barking wildly, due to all the excitement. Once things had calmed down, their mother pointed out that he would be their responsibility, they would have to look after him and take him for walks. She admitted he would be company while they were at school and when their father was away on business.

“The only reason we didn’t agree to a dog back in London was because there, we were out at work all day,” said father, laughing as Sooty washed his face, “as for being a guard dog,” he continued, “I think he would just lick any intruder to death, don’t you?”

Mum had found an old dog basket in the attic and placed it next to her desk in their office so giving Sooty a quiet corner to curl up in during the day.

The snow finally arrived, it fell thick and fast. Sooty could be seen chasing after the children on their sledges. He settled in quickly and was loved by all.

---

# Chapter 2

## Questions

The weather was improving and the snow gone, as the three children began to read the blue books, left for them by Uncle Seddie containing Anna's and Moley's stories. Moley was Anna's pet name for Sedgwick, her younger brother. The stories, they soon discovered, related to the year 1856, during the reign of Queen Victoria. Beth read aloud the first story of the era, written by Anna:-

*Moley (Sedgwick) and I made our first visit, in the new era, to St. George's Church. No one was around. The interior of the church looked very ornate and noticeably cheerful, even more so than in the Georgian period. We saw the most exquisitely embroidered altar cloth that sparkled with gold thread, on which stood an engraved brass cross, some candle sticks, along with an abundance of flowers, even though it was only February. I ran my fingers tips over the beautifully carved partitions and the highly polished pews which had been added close to the altar. I found little brass plates attached to them confirming these were for the sole use of various wealthy families. The many brightly coloured windows caused dappled patches of colour on the flagstones around the church. I made my way up the aisle to look at the patterns on the vividly embroidered kneelers that had caught my eye. As I bent over, I heard screeches of laughter from behind me. "Oh, Anna," said Moley, when he caught his breath, and dried his eyes, "you really mustn't bend over or you'll cause uproar if you do, especially in church. I was just treated to a full view of your underwear. Your frilly pantaloons are really very funny."*

*"Oh dear," I giggled, as I realised, that due to the hoops under the skirt the back had been lifted into the air, "awful, aren't they?" My skirt was a crinoline, wide and round, very much like a bell. "I will have to watch the other ladies and learn how to move about by copying their ways!"*

*Moley replied, in a mock posh voice. "You will have to learn to bend your knees and sink down gracefully, my dear," after which we both started to giggle.*

*"Do you think the vicar will be here soon?" I asked Moley.*

*"Who knows," he replied, "he could be away visiting the sick and he might be ages!"*

*"Oh well then, let's have a look on our own; we should be able to figure out where the graveyard has been extended since we were here last."*

*It was a chilly February morning. Even though the sun was shining brightly, the breeze was icy, making our faces tingle. We began to check around, moving amongst the tomb stones and clumps of white snowdrops. So intent were we on our purpose that we hadn't heard the vicar's approach, partly due to the noise of the seagulls screeching above us and the rooks crowing loudly.*

*"Good day to you. Can I be of any help?" offered a little man, dressed in black with a white collar from which hung two wide white pieces of what looked like ribbon, each some eight inches long, that flapped in the breeze. He had small eyes and mousey brown hair sticking out from under his wide-brimmed shallow domed hat.*

*"Oh, good morning, vicar," I replied, making my way over to him. I held out my hand, which he took briefly. "We were looking for the grave of an ancestor of ours, Jamie Pendleton."*

*"Really, when did he die?" he asked.*

*"That's something we don't know. He would have been about sixteen years old in 1755 so his date of birth would have been..."*

*"1739 June 2nd I believe," chimed in Moley, who was always good at arithmetic, as he offered his own hand to the vicar. "How do you do, I'm Sedgwick Pendleton, known to friends as Moley and this is my sister, Anna."*

*"Very pleased to meet you, I'm the Reverend John Barclay," he replied, "so if he died at any time from 1755 to say around 1839, when he would have been 100 years old, then his grave should be in that area there. However... if he was buried in someone's family plot, he could be anywhere. Perhaps we would be better off going indoors and checking the parish registers on this cold day. Come, let's see what we can find."*

*We followed him to the vicarage, where he arranged for tea, before taking us into his office, with its very large desk. The area behind the desk was rather cramped so that the vicar had to ease himself around it and into his chair. The room was filled with books and from one of the shelves, close to him, he lifted down two large and dusty registers. "Here, young man, would you check the one up to 1790 and I will check the later one." Just then the tea arrived and Mrs Grant, the housekeeper, placed the tray carefully on the desk before withdrawing. "Would you do me the honour of pouring tea for us, Miss Pendleton?"*

*"My pleasure," I replied and took off my short cape of wine coloured brocade, trimmed with cream satin cord and proceeded to pour out the tea. I remembered to sit on an armless chair, sitting carefully, so as to angle the skirt of my dress, so it did not rise up at the front and embarrass myself or shock the vicar.*

*As the checking was a long process, we stopped to sup our tea.*

*"You are strangers to the area?" asked the Vicar.*

*"Yes, we are, but we once had relatives who lived at Wattle Peak," replied Moley.*

*"Oh, the big Georgian house on the cliff. It's empty at present, just the caretaker there, I believe. He lives alone in the old farmhouse, in the grounds. Tell me more about James Pendleton?"*

*"James Pendleton was a teacher and ran a local school, built on an old farm not far from here." I explained. "From the cliff's edge on the farm you can see St Michael's Mount."*

*"Oh yes, I know the place. When the money ran out the parish council took it over and the children's home, built close by. It later became a workhouse, that was many years ago."*

*We finished checking the registers, but there was no entry for Jamie.*

*"He may have moved elsewhere and been buried in a different parish, so was it important to find him?" enquired the Reverend.*

*"No, it's more of a case of curiosity on our part," replied Moley. "The house at Wattle Peak, do you know if it's 'for let'?"*

*"You need to talk to the caretaker; he will know and arrange a visit for your parents, if they are interested. I warn you, he's a bit deaf; He took on the job a year ago."*

*We thanked the vicar for his help. He told us he would be pleased to see us anytime and to call on him for further help if we needed it. He said he knew everyone and where anything, we might need, could be found.*

*Moley and I made our way back to the farmhouse and knew now why it was so quiet there. Quickly, we entered the attic, I opened the lid of the trunk and the room whirled and the air sparkled. We arrived back in the attic, back in our own time within 15 seconds and removed our own clothes from the trunk and quickly got changed.*

*"I wish I knew what happened to Jamie, I miss him very much." I quickly wiped away a tear as we walked up to the main house once more. I couldn't bear to think of him as dead but knew it had to be. I hoped he had a good life without us, that perhaps he had moved to Exeter to be with Giles, but realised we might never know what happened to him.*

*We talked about the coming Spring of 1909, when our new guardian would arrive to take over from Step Aunt Wanda. Life promised to be so much better. "It was such a pity, Jamie would not be here to enjoy it," I remarked.*

*"Yes, but we weren't to know Wanda would be removed. If he hadn't gone, she would still have been in charge. No, he was safer back there in 1755, rather than perhaps dead in 1908 at the hands of that horrid woman," said Moley, with a shudder.*

*"I wonder why he hasn't left us a note as he promised? He said he would, and would place it in the gap under the window sill in the attic?"*

*"Humm... say he left a note for us four years after we said goodbye, then just maybe we would have to wait three years or so before we could find it.*

*"Because of the time difference, you mean." I replied. "Yes, that could be it, we know that we spend more time away in the past than has passed back at home, four hours there is only three in ours own time."*

*"We will just have to keep checking and hope, one day, we will find it."*

Beth closed the blue book with a sigh, "Poor Anna, it must have been hard for her. I wonder if they ever found out about Jamie's life and if he ever did leave a note. Let's check the hidey-hole tomorrow," said Beth, full of excited anticipation.

---

## Chapter 3

### The Victorians

"Come on, Sooty," called Jake, impatiently waiting to open the tack room door. The little dog scooted past as he opened it, leaving him to follow in his wake. He hurried up the stairs to where Mike had been busily sorting out the electric fire, and had switched it on.

It was the end of January 1982 and the attic was so cold that the youngsters could see their breath in the air. As the fire started to glow a cheerful red, the boys huddled over it while Beth stood with her back to them, attempting to prise out a piece of wood from behind the large wooden bracket that held up the window sill. On managing to remove the wood that Jamie had used to cover the gap, she shouted, "At last," then carefully lifted out a folded piece of paper, yellowed with age. "I'll read out what it says," she stated, making her way towards the others, who had seated themselves on the old comfortable garden chairs, positioned around the fire.

*Dear Anna and Moley*

*Just to let you know, I shall be leaving the country tomorrow. Giles has asked me, at extremely short notice, to go with him to his plantation in Jamaica. He wants me to open a school for the children of the plantation owners and overseers. I have agreed, as it is my chance to see the world.*

*After you left, I met a lovely girl called Lucinda. We were to marry, but just before my 21st birthday she contracted cholera and died.*

*You would be proud to learn that your big brother has not only been running the school, but also a home for orphaned and abandoned children. It is running well and gave both a purpose and much pleasure to my life, after losing Lucinda. I shall be leaving it all in good hands with a young man named Albert, who is an excellent teacher.*

*I hope to come back to Cornwall one day but cannot be sure that I will. I shall then have much more to tell you. I am keeping in good health and I pray that both of you are well and that your lives have changed for the better. Please do not worry about me, just imagine the adventures I shall have.*

*Your loving brother,*

*Jamie 4th June 1763.*

"There is a note on the reverse," added Beth.

"What does it say?" enquired Jake, "go on, read it out Beth."

"Okay, okay, hold on a mo."

*Dear Jamie,*

*All is well with us and after Wanda was eventually forced to leave Wattle Peak, we were looked after by mother's cousin,*

*Sarah Jane and she has been good to us. Good luck on your journey and have fun.*

*Love Anna and Moley - 2nd June 1913.*

*PS: If you do come back and get this note, please let us know more.*

“There’s no further message,” remarked Mike, after Beth passed him the paper. “So we don’t know if Jamie ever saw Anna and Moley’s reply. I somehow doubt that messages could go back in time. Anna and Moley got the note three years after we last saw Jamie and of course, well after their own last visit to the Georgian era finished, at the end of 1908.”

“Now we know why they were not likely to find his grave,” commented Jake and the other two nodded sadly in agreement.

“Shall we see what’s in the third trunk, then?” asked Beth, trying to lighten the mood.

Jake hurried over to take out the key from its little pocket in the second trunk. Soon they were wading through clothes and other objects relating to Victorian times. Beth found the cape worn by Anna with its matching dress, for winter use. The dress was in fact a skirt and top that matched perfectly. It had a tight bodice and loose sleeves, gathered at the wrists. The top sat neatly over the skirt. The neckline was high with a little rounded collar and there was pin-tuck pleating on the front panel, starting each side of the neck down to the waistline at the front, ending in points and edged with the satin cord. There was another top of pink satin, with a round neck and short frilly sleeves, embellished with the same rich cream coloured satin cord. The satin cord had been wound into various patterns and stitched on the skirt and cape. The second top was for social occasions. A wider band of the same cord could be seen above the frill at the skirt's hem. Her shoes were in fact bootees, which were fastened on one side with four small covered buttons. The bottom half of the boot was wine in colour and the top half cream. She had a matching wine-coloured hat, which was small, round and flat topped, measuring about 3 inches (7 centimetres) high and hanging from its back was a small piece of cream lace. There was a cream coloured fur muff on a cream cord to hang around her neck, ready to keep warm her hands.

They found boxes of matches, which Beth remembered, Great Uncle Sedgwick always referred to as 'Lucifers and. a lamp that was hung on what looked like a shepherd's-crook, the pole screwed together in the centre. There were two walking canes with fancy silver tops. The boys were pleased to find, this time, that they had long black narrow trousers to wear, instead of the short trousers and long silken hose, as in Georgian times. There were fancy waistcoats, with bronze satin backs, their fronts a silver grey brocade, that fastened with a double row of buttons at the front. These were to be worn over white collarless shirts of fine cotton with silk cravats at the neck. Their black jackets had a collar and lapels. Though the style of jacket remained on the long side, they were looser than before, the lower front being cut away in a slant from the waist and then rounded at the back with a slit.

At the bottom of the trunk were two top hats in black silk. One was slightly smaller so that it fitted inside the other, both in a special box. Mike and Jake put these on and picked up the canes. They started to saunter up and down admiring themselves in the tall mirror. Mike tipped his hat at a jaunty angle, and then pretended he had a long moustache, by miming at pulling and twiddling it into a point, before saying to Jake in his best upper class accent, “Top hole, old man, how goes it?”

Jake stopped and leant on his cane, joining in the game. “Spiffing, don’t you know,” he replied, in a similar accent. Beth clapped her hands in delight and grinned at the boys who were laughing.

There were short heavy capes in black and grey tweed with armholes, for the boys to wear over their suits. Beth left the summer clothes wrapped up for now and just hung up the winter outfits. Lifting out of the first of the trays, Beth found the usual jewellery box containing the odd pieces of jewellery plus a ruby pendant necklace. In addition, they found money: sovereigns and half-guineas, silver florins, shillings, small silver three-penny pieces and sixpences. There were purses and wallets for them to use and the boys both had watches on chains to attach to their waistcoats, “No more listening out for that church clock,” said Beth.

They decided, that on the following Saturday morning, they would venture into Victorian times and the boys left Beth enjoying sorting out all they would need for their adventure.

---

Chapter 4

## Down by the Sea

It was late morning as the room swirled and they entered the Victorian era. They noted that the attic now looked basically the same as in their own time, with the narrow room partitioned off from the main room, with its cupboards and hanging space. The children wondered whether these alterations had been made to house extra staff and provide them with their own storage. There were boxes and some ancient looking chairs.

They had left Sooty at home today. The boys decided to leave their top hats in the attic for now. Dressed in their splendid outfits, the trio made their way downstairs, their excitement mounting as they slowly opened the tack room door and carefully peered out. They noticed how quiet it was and there were weeds growing between the flag stones in the stable yard.

"Maybe it's still empty," said Beth as Jake went to check the stables.

"Yes, it's empty alright," Jake informed them, shrugging his shoulders, "no sign of any horses or feed, just some very old hay."

Crossing the courtyard, they investigated the small horse drawn carriage under the open barn. It was in need of repair and slightly different from the ones seen in Georgian times as it had springs attached to the body. "Hopefully, they will make it a more comfortable ride," remarked Mike, "Do you remember that journey to Hayle with Mrs Wainwright? I'll never forget that, although it was a wonderful day, it was a rough and bumpy ride."

"Don't remind me," said Beth, "I ached all over the next day."

Over they went to the side gate. Mike pulled a face as it squeaked loudly when opened and again as he closed it after them. "Let's hope it's still the same old caretaker. Weren't Anna and Moley told he was somewhat deaf?" said Mike.

It was a misty day, the sea hardly visible as they peered down the cliff path leading down to the beach.

"Oh, look, the iron railings have now been added to the outer edge where the path narrows," said Beth, "I had wondered how old they might be."

"I wonder how they fitted them?" said Mike "I can see part of the metal work has been attached to the cliff face below the path. You'd need a good head for heights to work over the side, dangling down the cliff as you did so."

"It's the age of engineering work; don't you remember our teacher telling us about the iron foundries, the iron ship and the bridges of Isambard Kingdom Brunel?" declared Beth. Britain was a major manufacturer and Queen Victoria was on the throne.

They walked quickly along the cliff top road before veering off onto the road leading to the village. Looking around, Beth said, "it's much bigger now, the village certainly has grown since 1760."

"A lot more side roads, I've counted six so far and most of the new houses are built of brick. It is more of a small town now," said Mike.

In the Square there were more shops. They peered into the green-grocers with its selection of vegetables and fruit alongside the general store. A well-stocked book shop sat next to the ironmongers selling pots, pans, kettles and there was even a post office. The milliners on the far side caught Beth's eye, as it now had an extra window selling ready-made clothes and they even had a sewing machine on sale that you turned by hand and another that could be used with a foot treadle.

The smell of fresh bread from the bakers had Jake hurrying into the shop. He emerged five minutes later with a box of cakes. "They're for later," he said grinning, as the others shook their heads at him.

Entering the bookshop, Mike began to search through the books, while Beth looked at the stationery section, where the visiting cards, invitation and pretty dance cards took her eye. Jake was pleased to see there were newspapers on sale. He told

Beth he was keen to know what was going on in the area, so bought a copy of the 'The Cornish Times'. He tucked it under his arm beneath his cape, as the other two indicated they were ready to leave.

Mike disappeared and returned, having picked up a bottle of lemonade from the store. They decided to visit the small harbour, some five minutes away. The mist had lifted by the time they sat on the harbour wall, looking around in the weak and hazy sunshine. The fishermen had already sold off their catch. Their empty boxes lay around and the men sat smoking their pipes, the blue smoke could be seen steadily rising as they mended their nets. Others busily sorted out their boats. There was a fishy smell in the air. Seagulls wheeled overhead as the trio tucked into their cakes. "Umm, these are lovely Jake," said Beth, as she leant over to one side to try and prevent crumbs landing on her skirt.

Holding the lemonade bottle between his knees, Mike pulled back the wire clamps that held the stopper in place and handed the bottle around. No sooner had they finished drinking it, than a bare footed ragged urchin appeared pleading to have the empty bottle. Mike happily gave it to him and watched the lad run off and appeared puzzled, as to why the boy seemed so mightily pleased with himself. "Oh, Mike," said Beth smiling, "of course he was pleased, there was a halfpenny deposit to be refunded on its return, didn't you see the sign in the store?"

"No, I didn't?" said Mike, "oh well, I'm sure he could do with the money."

"The mist could be coming in again," said Jake, as he stood up and stretched.

"Yes, you're right and it's about time we started back, the daylight will be gone shortly," replied Beth.

Turning, they noticed on the other side of the harbour, high on the beach where it flattened out, two large odd looking long wooden constructions. "They remind me of a barrel that had been cut in half length-ways with its open belly laid on the ground and then cut in half again across the middle," said Mike, "how weird, I've never seen a barrel so huge."

The wider ends were angled slightly so they were not directly facing the sea. Strangely, the tops or roofs were rounded and came to a point whereas the back ends, one tapered to a point, whereas the other was blunter.

"Yes, very strange," said Beth, "there's definitely something familiar about them, we've just time to check them out."

While they picked their way over the sand and rocks to take a look they saw an old lady ahead of them making her way along the beach. As they caught up with her she moved to stand in front of the first of the wooden buildings. The flat front contained a door. The grey haired old lady was dressed in a woollen shawl, dark skirt and poke bonnet with a frill that hung down from back hem down her neck. She turned slowly and asked if she could help them?

"We were just curious to see what the buildings were," said Mike shyly. "We hope you don't mind us taking a closer look?"

She gave a chuckle, "You're not the first to be curious," she said, "come and I'll tell you about it, if you have five minutes to spare," so they followed her as she took them around to the other side where they could see a tin chimney sticking out on the side and where there were several windows.

"It's a house!" said Jake surprised.

There was a bench in front of the windows and the old lady indicated to Beth to sit down with her. Once seated, the old lady took out of her pocket a small white clay pipe and filled the bowl before lighting it.

"Some fifty years ago there were many smugglers in these parts. It was a very profitable business back then. Some ships and schooners were built with double hulls, to hide the smuggled goods inside. If the smugglers were caught, their boats were confiscated and broken up, as a lesson to others. Some of the schooners were stripped of all saleable trimmings and then their hulls were cut in half so they could never go to sea again. That is what we have here."

"Of course," said Beth, 'it's the two halves of a schooner's hull. We just don't see that much of a boat unless it's out of water and certainly never upside down. Wow!"

"Aye Lass, you've got it, this was once a fine schooner named the 'Mary Ellen'. We bribed a customs officer to let us know when they were going to carry out the work on it, so we could lay claim to one half. My parents and brothers, some of whom were carpenters, set about carefully turning the hull over, then boarded up the front and added a door and windows, thus making it into a fairly roomy house. I'll admit, it's a very strange shape," she laughed, "but it's been a good home. As long as we tar between the boards and give it a coat of varnish, it will last many years yet and of course it's waterproof. The house has a pot belly stove for heating and cooking, making it warm and snug in winter and there is plenty of drift wood found along the beach for fuel. There's only me and one brother left now, although at one time eight of us lived here."

"So is your half, Mary or Ellen?" asked Jake with a chuckle, making them all smile.

"Don't mind him," said Beth, as she gave her brother a playful nudge, adding, "I see you only have windows on one side?"

"Yes, the winds are fierce in winter and tend to batter the windowless side of the hull. On occasions the waves, during a bad storm, have even come right up to it, so that is why we found it prudent to make it just as you see it, not quite facing the sea," and gave them a rueful smile.

They thanked her for her kindness and started back, just as the light was beginning to fade. Leaving the beach they stopped to shake the sand from their feet and, on looking up, the sun was low in the sky. It resembled a fuzzy pink ball.

They walked back into the village and through the Square. Beth noticed down a side street, two dark shapes in the distance. As she peered into the mist it lifted slightly and she could make out the two characters, their backs to her. One was tall and the other was slight and smaller. The taller one had on what looked like a battered top hat crushed to one side, the small one's short trouser bottoms were ragged, his short jacket was not much better, the sleeves reaching only halfway down his forearm. His limbs were very black as was his hair. Was he an African boy, she wondered? She could see the boy carried what looked like a bunch of poles, the ends sticking up into the air. It was then that she noticed the rope tied to the boy's waist and the other end in the tall man's hand, the latter's long coat tails flapped a little as he walked. Beth turned to tell the boys about it but as she looked down the road the mist had swallowed everything once more. "Mike, am I right in thinking that slavery was abolished during early Victorian times?" asked Beth.

"Yes, why do you ask?"

"I thought I saw a black boy tethered by a rope to a man, in that side road just before the mist descended again."

"Perhaps you did, we will keep an eye out for them, we're bound to come across them again sometime," Mike replied.

They hurried on through the outskirts of the village towards the farmhouse. The swirling mist gave the trees an eerie feel. Once they got near to the cliff road they kept a close eye on the path. It could be dangerous in dense mist. Soon they were in the attic and travelled back to their own time, where they quickly changed into their own everyday clothes, glad to be out of the damp air.

It wasn't at all misty at home, just a dark cold February evening, with the glistening frost crunching under their feet, as they hurried back to the main house knowing tea would be ready for them and an excited Sooty would be there to greet them. Beth suddenly stopped, "Oh no, we forgot to find out the year we were in," she cried, cross with herself.

"Won't that newspaper I bought, but left in our attic, help?" asked Jake.

"Well done, Jake, we will check it tomorrow," replied Mike, ruffling his brother's unruly blonde hair.

---

# Chapter 5

## The Newspaper

The following day, Jake picked up the Victorian newspaper and hurried back home. He scooted up the stairs to Beth's room, where she and Mike waited, where her colourful posters of her favourite pop star, Adam Ant, stared down at them. The room was cosy and so much warmer than their attic. The newspaper, they saw, was dated 30th January 1860.

Armed with this knowledge, Beth quickly headed for the library. She sorted through the books until she found the house accounts for 1860. Pleased, she hurried back and lifted down from a shelf, the new diary that she intended to use to enter useful notes from the accounts, their great uncles books, as well as details of their own adventures. The boys were busy reading through the newspaper. Beth could see there were no photos, but many drawings, mostly relating to adverts.

A full page article about a forthcoming 'Grand Market' to be held on 25th March with its attractions and 'Hiring Fair' had caught their attention. "That's 'Lady Day' when the landlords are in town to gather their quarterly rents." stated Mike, "the village will be really busy."

Beth had checked the house accounts for the first few months. The only entries were for the weekly wages of the caretaker and that of the cleaner every other week, plus a few entries for cleaning materials, so she left the rest of the accounts to read and note up later.

"Have you seen this?" said Jake, pointing to where the newspaper gave a timetable for the general market in towns and villages around the county. It showed that it came to Pennington on the first Tuesday of every month.

"It's probably mainly for the farmers, with their livestock," said Beth, what with all the different shops that have sprung up in Pennington, there would be no need for a general weekly market anymore."

"Yes, you might be right but on the 25th March it's a 'Grand Market' and has quite a bit to see according to the list of stalls selling crafts, pottery, fabrics and fancy goods, imported items, small rugs, brassware and exotic spices," said Mike, "and many other attractions it says."

"Also a wide variety of cheeses from all over Cornwall and Devon," Jake added.

"Grand Market, it does sound like a good day to visit," said Beth and the others agreed eagerly.

Beth was fascinated by the newspaper's advertisements, offering various sorts of medicines, pills and potions, all of which made the most fantastic claims. If only the cures were true, she thought.

One advert, for a hair pad, was a stroke of luck for Beth as she realised she had one in the trunk and now knew how to use it. Apparently, it was fastened to your head with a comb and you hid it under a layer of hair before pinning the rest of your hair over it, in curls, thereby enabling you to raise your hair style higher. She had wondered how they managed the styles and found the diagrams in the newspaper were a great help.

"Look at all the notices for house sales and auctions of household goods, next to the notices of death, births and pending marriages," said Jake.

"You should read the next page. It shows details of recent criminal trials and of court cases shortly to come before the magistrates. It's quite frightening, the sentences that are still being handed out for minor crimes," said Mike, shaking his head and handing the paper to Beth.

They were all eager to go adventuring, but March 25th seemed such a long way off, so they decided to visit once more on Saturday, at the end of February to check out the mine.

On Saturday morning they set off, back to the Victorian era. Quietly, they left the tack room and approached the side gate. There Mike told Beth and Jake to hold on a minute and they watched as he took a candle from his pocket and rubbed the wax into the gate hinges while moving it back and forth, until the squeaking stopped.

"That was clever," said Beth, "where did learn about that?"

"I asked dad, of course," he replied smugly.

Walking along the cliff top road Jake and the dog ran on ahead. Jake was enjoying throwing sticks for Sooty, but stopped and waited for the others when he got close to the mine. They noted the mine was as busy as ever. They sat down on a mossy bank to watch for a while the scene spread out below them.

"Something's different," said Beth puzzled.

"Yes, there are no small children," said Jake, "I spotted that straight away."

"No women either," said Mike amazed. "There are still some boys about ten or eleven years old, I would say."

"Thank goodness some things have changed for the better," said Beth, "it was a horrible way to earn a living. I know from checking ahead in my history textbook, there was some government legislation in 1833 to do with factories. That's something you and I, Mike, will be studying later this year."

They moved further along the road that skirted the mine and saw a wheel house for pumping water out from the mine, by means of a steam engine.

The little street of miners' houses was still there and had even been extended. Thankfully, there was no sign of the open sewer that caused the dreadful illness in the last century.

"There's even a little general store in the street, but I must say the people seem no better off than back in Georgian times. Even the style of their clothes seemed hardly to have changed, the poor are still so shabbily dressed," remarked Beth.

"They're still thin," said Jake, as two men with shoulders hunched over proceeded down the street.

They rose and headed on towards the church. To their surprise, when it came into view, a wedding party was just leaving. Beth stood looking at the bride, who wore a blue dress and a lace shawl with a circle of real flowers in her hair. The bride, looking quite radiant, turned towards them and smiled. The happy guests prepared to walk back to the village with the bride and groom walking under a wicker canopy covered in flowers mostly lily of the valley and yellow primula. There was much laughter, as rice and petals were scattered around by the wedding party as it moved off and everyone began singing and clapping to a lively tune played on a penny whistle. The vicar stood smiling and waved them off, before he suddenly noticed the trio who stood watching.

"Hello there, are you part of the wedding party? If so they are off to the King's Head for the wedding breakfast."

"No, we're not," said Beth, "we just came to look at the church. We were told by our cousins, who came here a few years back, that it's very old and fine."

"Well, I have to say I'm rather proud of it. I'm the Reverend Barclay and I'm always happy to welcome newcomers to the church. I must admit, you will find it looks quite resplendent today as it has been decked out with flowers for the wedding."

"The Reverend Barclay, did you say?"

"Why yes, you have heard of me?" he said astonished.

"Yes," said Beth smiling, "through family, Anna and Moley, sorry Sedgwick Pendleton, mentioned you. You may remember them, they asked you about a relative, Jamie

Pendleton, who, they thought, was buried here many years ago? Oh, I'm sorry we should have introduced ourselves. These are my brothers Mike and Jake and I'm Beth Robertson. That little rascal over there, rolling in the grass is Sooty. Here boy!" Sooty scampered over and sat by her side.

"Well I never, I do remember them, in fact I saw them several times while they visited the area. They made a generous gift to the poor box before they finally left.

"Why not have lunch with me? It's nice to see some new faces. The groom has left me a dozen eggs and half a ham, as part payment for performing the wedding service. I'm sure my cook, Mrs Grant, will rustle something up, meantime why not have a look around the church and come across when you are ready. Shall I take Sooty for you?"

"That's very kind of you, thank you," said Beth, as Jake gave the vicar a beaming smile. 'Jake must be getting hungry,' thought Beth, as she placed Sooty on his lead and handed it to the vicar, as they prepared to enter the church. Sooty, on his best behaviour, trotted alongside the vicar into the vicarage.

A little later they all sat around the vicar's parlour with its red and cream striped wall paper and heavy red velvet curtains framing the windows. The roaring fire, so inviting, made the room very cosy.

A white tablecloth edged with lace covered the table close to the window. On this, was placed, a platter of buttered bread and a Victoria sponge cake, on a raised glass dish. When the cook-cum-housekeeper, Mrs Grant, entered, she brought in plates of ham and poached eggs. All three couldn't wait to tuck in. The tea pot sat ready to pour and Beth remembered to use the tea strainer, as there were no teabags in Victorian times.

It was a splendid lunch. The Reverend Barclay was very jolly and good company, as well as being a knowledgeable person, as they soon realised. Beth asked him about the mine, telling him that she was dismayed to have seen young boys working there.

"The miners, yes, you would have seen boys 10 years old and over and men but no females, as that was changed by the 1842 Act, thank goodness."

"Oh, I thought the rules changed in 1833," said Beth puzzled.

"Not for the miners! The 1833 Act related only to some factories, linen mills and the like. It was brought about by the efforts of the reformers, such as Lord Shaftesbury. They published details of the terrible working conditions in factories. They told how the children had to climb under working machinery, that many were killed or hurt when sheer exhaustion made them clumsy. The overseers cruelly forbade the children to rest during their long shifts just so they could keep up the production levels for their masters. In fact, if the poor mites fell asleep when they should have been working, they didn't get paid at all and were even beaten."

"How could people be so cruel?" cried Jake.

"Quite so lad," added the vicar. "The 1833 Act went some way to prevent the injuries as the starting age was raised to nine years in the factories and textile mills. Inspectors were brought in to enforce these rules, along with two hours education per day. However, Parliament absolutely refused to include the miners in the Act, claiming that the country could not afford it!"

"I think that was quite wicked. It's hard to believe that Parliament failed to right these matters earlier," added Mike.

"You would have thought so. However, the rich and powerful owners of factories and mines have fought the reforms every step of the way and it didn't help that many owners were actually members of Parliament."

Just then, there was a knock on the door and Mrs Grant entered "Alright to clear away now, Sir?" she asked, holding a tray ready to clear the table.

"Please do," he replied and the children helped collect the plates together for her, as they thanked her for a lovely meal. Jake asked if he could have the sponge cake recipe. Cook was as pleased as punch and promised to write it down for him.

As they settled down once more, the Reverend Barclay said "Now, where was I… oh yes, but maybe you have had enough of all that?"

“Oh please, go on with what you were saying,” urged Mike, “I really want to know more,” and the other two nodded and smiled encouragingly.

“It wasn’t until 1842 that the Government was shamed into bringing in changes for the mines, relating to women and boys less than 10 years.”

“Shamed?” asked Beth

“Yes, my dear. It was as result of Lord Shaftesbury’s ‘Commission on Child Labour in Mines’. set up in 1840. It was read out in the Houses of Parliament, stating all the shocking and dreadful details of conditions under which the miners, including children as young as five and women, were forced to work, along with the dangers. Even some MPs had tears in their eyes by the end of it.

“There was another Factories Act in1844 that reduced the hours for women to 12 hours, the same as for children and young persons aged 13-18.

The reformers fought for a 10 hour working day and in 1847 it came about, but not adult males. However, there was a loophole in the law and the factory owners started to bring in a relay system.”

“What was that then?” enquired Jake.

“The owners forced the women, children and young persons, to stay in the factory for the whole of the 15 hour shift worked by the men so there was a constant supply of materials to pass to the men. They stood down women and young persons for periods in the morning or in the afternoon, to suit their production needs. They were careful, ensuring they only worked a total of ten hours each. Of course they only paid them for 10 hours, despite being made to stay there for 15 hours. Certainly not what the 10 hour rule was meant to do."

"What a callous thing to do," said Mike. "Surely they couldn't get away with that?"

"I'm afraid so, but then Lord Shaftesbury stepped in to try and stop all the manufacturers bringing in the same bad practice. He worked on a compromise with the employers."

"In 1850 working hours of children were reduced to 6 ½ a day instead of 9, but in return the women and young persons would work 10 ½ instead of 10, restricted to between the hours of 6am to 6pm each day and everyone would only work up to 2pm on Saturdays.

"Unfortunately, another condition of the Act was that young children would start to work in factories at the age of eight years instead of nine, so a case of two steps forward and one step back, I would say," the vicar sighed.

"I don't suppose the women and young persons were very pleased at having to work an extra half hour per day, even if they did gain Saturday afternoon off," commented Mike.

"No indeed, the workers fell out with Lord Shaftesbury over that, so his Lordship now concentrates his efforts on the other industries not covered by any of the Acts, such as the potteries, dyeing and bleach works and lace makers, to name a few.

"I still think the 6 ½ hours' work for those children is a very long period," said Beth, shaking her head.

"I agree with you my dear," said the vicar. "But I remember the bad old days, when children as young as five worked for up to 16 hours a day in the mines and factories. It makes me want to weep, when I think about what I saw back then, as a young man. It was pitiful to watch the little ones in the early hours, as they were carried to work asleep on their parent's backs or on those of their older siblings and brought home again the same way, after the long working day had finished."

"That sounds like no life at all," sighed Beth.

"Yes, you're right, Beth," replied the vicar.

"Jake told me that you, Beth and Mike, will be 14 years old in a few months," said the Reverend. Can you image yourselves working in a factory ten and half hours a day with only a break of one hour for food. And, Jake, I don't think you'd like it if you were forced to work in the mine six and half hours a day just so you could have barely enough to eat."

Jake shook his head and shuddered. "No, I wouldn't, all that hard work and misery for so little reward." He looked glum. Beth thought that Jake might be feeling a little guilty that he had eaten so much, while so many went hungry.

"I do hope that soon things will improve for the children. It's wrong that they should have to work at all," said Beth.

"We pray so, but whether one day we can prevent all children working," the vicar sighed and shrugged his shoulders, "I simply don't know. All we can do is to carry on trying to improve conditions, however long it takes. It is nice to know that children of your social standing have concerns about such matters."

"Our parents are keen that we understand what goes on in the world," replied Mike, looking bleak.

"It does your parents credit and they're no doubt proud of you all," remarked the vicar smiling as he replaced his cup back on its saucer.

"Well, let's talk about something more cheerful. Are you staying here for good or just visiting?"

"We shall be around the area for about a year," said Mike. "We are staying nearby in Torrington and visiting various places."

"Well, I'm just about to put up a notice in the church porch about the trip to St Ives for the May Day celebrations. Would you like to come? There will be several wagons going. It's usually good fun and there will be maypole dancing, Morris Men, hobby horses and other shows at the fair. I'm sure you would enjoy it."

"Yes please," said Beth, and the others nodded their heads in agreement.

"What's a hobby horse?" asked Jake.

"Let's see if I can describe it for you. It's an oblong wooden frame with a wooden horse's head at the front and tail at the back, of course, with a hole in the middle where the man wearing it stands. The frame is held up by straps over his shoulders and the whole frame is covered by cloth that reaches to the ground, so you can't see the man's legs. The wearer is dressed as a knight and there are legs painted on the side of the cloth, so he appears to be riding on the horse. It is beautifully decorated in medieval fashion. They really do look splendid."

"Any chance I could have a go at pretending to be a knight on a charger?" said Jake, obliviously taken with the idea.

"I doubt it, Jake, they are expensive to make and the owner makes his living using it. He, with the others in his troupe, visit towns all around the country."

"That's settled then," said the vicar, "I shall look forward to your company on May Day," as he added their names to the list.

"Thank you for our lunch," said Beth, "but we must start back as it looks like rain."

"Oh my, you could be right, it does look a bit black," said the vicar, while helping Beth on with her cape. Call again, won't you and if I can be of any help, you only have to ask."

The children and Sooty hurried into the village, as the first heavy drops began to fall, they made their way out onto the road, leading to the farmhouse. As they made their way down the lane they stopped to shelter under the trees waiting for the rain to ease, the wind whipping at the trees and bushes around them. These were mostly rather bare but with some shoots just appearing. They noticed, in the distance, the old caretaker making his way into the main house at Wattle Peak as they hurried on once more.

Carefully, the children checked around, in case the caretaker was on his way back to the farmhouse. All four were quite wet by the time they made it up to the attic and opened the trunk to travel home and very happy to get into their own clothes, before hanging up the soaking wet garments to dry.

When they got back indoors, their mother looked at them, surprised. “I hadn’t noticed it raining, you had better go and dry that damp hair. I’ll see to Sooty, here boy, you are a very bedraggled little lad,” and she smothered him in an old towel and rubbed him dry all the while he was trying to lick her face, making her laugh.

---

# Chapter 6

## Grand Market and Fair

March 25th was a school holiday. The trio changed into their Victorian costumes and hurriedly opened the lid of the trunk, impatiently waiting for the sparkling to stop. Sooty was with them as they set out for their day at a Victorian market and fair. The day was cool and the sunshine weak, so they were glad of their warm clothes.

As they approached the Square they saw there were many booths and show tents to visit.

"Look at the signs over the tents," said Jake 'The Fattest Man in the World' and the 'Bearded Lady'. Both of these had queues waiting for the next show as had the 'Mermaid' and the 'Flea Circus tents. The fortune teller sat by the entrance to her booth wearing a headscarf with many silver coins attached around its edge. The Square was very crowded as they nudged their way through.

"If we get split up we should meet by the King's Head Inn at 1pm." called out Mike, as he pushed on through the throng to where the fire eater and jugglers stood.

There was plenty more to see they realised as they neared the field opposite the church, where livestock and ponies were for sale. There was a butcher's stall where the carcasses of rabbits and hares were hung up for sale. Beth watched, as a woman picked one out and waited, while the butcher expertly removed the fur almost in one piece and placed it in a box ready to be made into collars, muffs and the like.

By lunchtime, the weather had improved and the sunshine lifted Beth's spirits. That was until she spotted the little black boy sitting on the ground by the beer table. He sat next to the man with his battered top hat. Both had their backs to her. The man cuffed the lad's head when he held out his hand and asked for another crust of bread. She saw the lad wince and as he turned towards her, she noted with sorrow, white streaks had appeared down his face where his tears ran. Then soot fell from his hair as he bent his head to wipe away the tears with his sleeve. 'He's a sweep's boy,' she gasped. He started coughing, holding his chest as he did so. He received another cuff to his head, as the man yelled at him to be quiet. Something at the back of her mind told Beth this should not be so. She hurried off frowning to find Mike and to tell him what she had seen.

Cream teas, sweets and the roasted nuts stalls had caught Jake's eye and with money at the ready, he was wandering happily from stall to stall, with Mike in tow when Beth caught up with them. Beth followed them and they seated themselves on an incline in front of the 'Punch and Judy' booth, with its red and white striped covering. The next show was about to start and Jake was busy breaking up a honeycomb, which he shared with them during the show. Meanwhile, Sooty gnawed contently on a bone, brought back by Beth from the butcher's stall. The show was very much as they remembered from their own time. However, to her surprise, the audience at times jeered or booed loudly when Punch appeared on stage They made jokes, to which Punch or Judy would reply, everyone enjoying the good- natured banter.

"I remember a crocodile eating the sausages," said Jake, "but there was none of that in this performance. Maybe, such a creature had not been seen yet or perhaps they simply weren't well known."

When the show had finished, Beth told them about the sweep's boy. Mike's face grew dark, before replying, "I'm sure boys sweeping chimneys was outlawed in the last century. Let's go and tackle the man about it, he must be stopped, it's so cruel. We could threaten to have the law set on him." Just then a man approached them to collect the fee of one half penny that they owed for the Punch and Judy show.

"Oh no, my purse and my money has gone," cried Beth, realising a hole had been cut in her bag, just big enough for the purse to fall out.

"Cut-purses and pick-pockets must be working around here today," said Mike, checking for his own money, relieved to find it safe.

"I think it was the man next to me by the butcher's stall," said Beth angrily, "he kept knocking into me, so he's the most likely suspect. We could go find a policeman, I saw one earlier. We could get him to search the man," said Beth, annoyed that she hadn't been aware of what was happening to her.

"You may be right," said Mike, "but if you are and the man was caught, he could end up being hanged. You read the magistrate's court reports in the newspaper Jake bought, stealing remains a hanging offence"

"Oh yes, you're right," she replied, "I'll just have to be more careful in future," sighed, Beth, "I wouldn't like to be the cause of someone's death, simply for stealing my purse."

The beer table was in sight but there was no sign of the sweep or his boy. While they looked about for them, they saw the Reverend Barclay approaching.

"Hello there, why the long faces?" he said cheerfully.

"Well," said Beth, "I was concerned to see a sweep with a boy who had obviously been crawling up a chimney, wasn't that outlawed many years ago?"

"Ah, I see. Come over here away from listening ears," replied the vicar, in a low voice. As they huddled round, he whispered, "You are right young lady but what can we do when the local judge has his own chimneys swept by the boy? If a charge is made against the sweep the judge would just dismiss it, otherwise he too could be charged. The owners of all the large old houses, unless they have had their chimneys rebuilt, find it better to have them cleaned that way. No one is willing to stand up to the judge. Houses built since the Act, in the late eighteenth century, have mostly had the new style of chimney with small flues."

"That poor boy, he was coughing pitifully," explained Beth, shaking her head. "I felt so sorry for him."

"It's the soot that gets into their lungs. Even when such boys become to large to fit up the chimney many do not live long, I'm afraid. The damage has already been done." The vicar then shrugged his shoulders wearily, resigned to the fact, "Such was the way of his world."

"Why don't I treat you all too some lemonade in the tea tent?" he suggested, as he took Beth's arm and led them over the rough grass, with Sooty chasing close behind. While Beth was busy telling him about the loss of her purse, the boys set about finding a table and benches for them all.

Later, when the children were alone once more, Mike purchased pies for them to eat, before they made their way towards the boxing tent, but there they were turned away.

"Children not allowed," stated a man, who collected the entrance fees, "why don't you go over there to the hall of mirrors?"

Having made their way over to the tent indicated and paying a half penny each to enter, they found the tent was really mostly a large screened off area mainly open to the sky, "No doubt to let in the light," explained Mike. There were partitions separating the mirrors. Each mirror showed you looking rather strange. Beth laughed, when looking at the first, as she appeared eight feet tall and very skinny. The next made them look extremely fat, here Beth moved, so that she could look over Jake's shoulder, "One day, you will look like that if you keep on eating," she said and tickled him, until he squealed for her to stop.

They rounded the next partition and giggled to see themselves with wide legs and tiny bodies. Another mirror made their heads look really big and they screamed with laughter as they saw each other's reflection. Then they found a large and wide mirror that was able to show all three of them at the same time, but each with a slightly different shape.

"Let's look around them all again," said Jake and they follow him back to each mirror, once more, to spend a while pulling faces until their sides hurt with so much laughing. The final section of the tent was one to be entered one at a time. Beth went first and found within that it was very puzzling. There were many mirrors placed at different angles, resulting in her image being reflected over and over again. Whichever way she turned, once she entered the maze, it seemed there were hundreds of images of her, making her confused as she turned this way and that and tried to find where each mirror actually ended. This left her needing to feel her way through and it was difficult to find the way out. Some turnings were dead ends and it was very confusing, leaving her unsure which way to turn for the exit.

"Well, that was fun," said Jake, when he finally made it out to find the other two. By then it was early evening, the sun was setting, bringing a chill to the air.

"We should start back," said Mike reluctantly, "we have not brought a lamp with us."

Strung out along the roadway, they trudged back to the farmhouse. Sooty, running back and forth, as if checking they were all there and he seemed still to have plenty of energy, whereas they were all quite tired. Beth was wondering, if the May Day trip would be half as much fun.

---

## Chapter 7

### May Day

The first of May seemed to arrive very quickly, thought Beth, but then again since the fair they had all been so busy over the weeks. Mike had been practising his bowling, hoping to get into the school's cricket team, but he wasn't chosen, though his name was on the reserve list. While Jake's last rugby match left him nursing a black eye, from a blow from someone's elbow, but he did score a try. With the rugby season over, Jake told Beth he was looking forward to supporting his dad at the local cricket matches on the village green. "Oh yes," she said, "nothing to do with enjoying the afternoon teas provided by the team members' wives, I suppose." Jake grinned.

Beth realised just how much of her time had been taken up by the various after school clubs and the drama group. Then again, she had also captained the netball team for a while, when her friend Sara had been ill. And she still managed to run the school's unofficial Adam Ant's fan club, her favourite pop star.

Off they set as soon as the sparkling had stopped. Excited, but cautiously they left the attic knowing they were in good time to meet the group heading to St Ives. They saw the group gathering on the green near the church and inspected the four lined up wagons each being able to hold ten persons. These contained bales of hay for everyone to sit on and were garlanded with greenery and flowers.

"Have you been and paid your respects to the May Queen?" asked the vicar, when he saw them standing by the last wagon. "You need to go and bow or curtsy to the May Queen. She is one of our local girls."

They duly made their way to the first wagon. Beth saw that the girl wore a blue velvet cloak over a white dress decorated with silk ribbons of many colours and a few sequins.

"Good day, your Majesty," said Beth, as she curtsied and her brothers bowed. "I do like your crown of flowers." Beth was quite envious of the beautiful headdress of pink and white roses that sat on the pretty girl's fair hair.

Soon they were all seated and the wagons set off. Jake took out of his pocket his penny whistle that he'd got from Jimmy back in puritan times and he played the tune, 'Ten Green Bottles', one of the few he had mastered. They soon had everyone singing the song, which appeared new to the others. The day was warm and the sun shone for most of the time. The hawthorn was in full flower as were the apple trees in the orchards. The woods were ablaze with many shades of green and the birdsong was very noticeable whenever there was a break in their own singing.

Several persons took turns at singing songs as they travelled through the lanes and along the highway. Beth said she was surprised just how much smoother the ride was now they had joined the main highway. “That’s due to the new road surfacing produced by Mac Adam a much more comfortable ride,” explained the vicar. It was some two hours later that they met up with several other wagon parties, from different villages, awaiting their turn to enter the town of St Ives and to make their way to the town’s Green.

“The May Queens from each of the villages are to be judged as to who is the fairest of them all and the remaining May Queens will take part in the Maypole dancing,” the Reverend Barclay told Beth.

On the Green they could see a dais had been set up with a throne upon it and in front of this was the Maypole, with its long ribbons of many colours. Nearby were some tents where tea, cakes and cider were available.

The vicar told them to run along and enjoy themselves, but to be back by the wagons by 4 o’clock at the latest ready for the journey home. “Do be sure to go down to the harbour at 1pm for the parade,” he called after them.

They moved carefully through the packed cobbled streets of St Ives as some lanes were so steep in places they became wide steps. They passed down the alleys and many small turnings to reach the harbour side, where the boats, decked with coloured flags, bobbed on the water. Bonfires were set up on the beach where you could buy potatoes to bake on the fire. Pats of butter along with slices of cheese were provided to go in them. Cooked prawns were cheap as were the oysters, so the children bought some for their lunch and brought them back in newspaper to where their potatoes were baking.

They sat on the sand holding rough pottery bowls containing their hot potatoes stuffed with butter and cheese. While these cooled off they ate the prawns and Mike opened the oysters with his pen knife and handed one to Beth, who swallowed it as instructed. She pulled a face, “Oh, I don’t think I want any more of them.”

“Okay, more for us,” said Jake, as Mike handed him the next one. From where they sat eating they could watch the Morris men dancing on the beach at the point where the sand evened out at low tide. The men were wearing white trousers and shirts with bells tied around their calves and above their elbows. Their first dance was with silk handkerchiefs held between them in two lines, five men each side, their bells jingling merrily. The next dance was with sticks as they formed a circle and tapped the sticks together, throwing them to one another as they danced to and fro, before ending up locking the sticks together to form a wheel shape that was then held on high.

“Wasn’t that last bit very clever?” remarked Mike. The others agreed. After their lunch was finished, they returned their bowls and collected their deposit. Jake looked up sharply. “That sounds like a horn,” said Mike.

“Let’s follow the sound,” replied Jake. Soon they were heading away from the harbour and entering a wide street nearby. There they saw a man in a long white robe with antlers attached to his head. He blew into a curly ram's horn once more and the procession moved off with him in the lead. The May Queens followed next as they set off to the Green. Men carrying hobby horses, who were dressed in their knights' costumes, just as the vicar had described them, followed them. The knights pretended to charge the crowd, to the squeals of the young children. Next was a man playing a merry tune on a tabor. This was a pipe with a drum attached to the side. The Morris men then joined the group ready to dance their way through the streets, followed by actors dressed in medieval costumes, ready to perform a short pageant. The procession wended its way with the crowds and children following in its wake.

Once back at the Green, the leading May Queen was led up to the dais to take her place on the throne. Unfortunately, she was not the girl from their village. The crowd clapped, as the Mayor placed a metal crown on her head. The other May Queens left her side to pick up their ribbons attached to the maypole and started to dance, as the fiddlers played. The girls weaved their way in and out around the pole so that it formed a pretty pattern, as the ribbons were wrapped around.

The children followed the crowd over to the Green for the country dancing, as people arranged themselves in set squares of eight. After watching for a short while, they realised these were easy to do. No one minded when someone made a mistake, they just laughed, so all three joined in.

Quite out of breath after several dances, Beth and the boys followed the actors to see the medieval play. The hobby horses were used in a mock jousting match, the chief knight saving the fair lady from a wicked lord by winning the joust and finally, a sword fight. A jester wandered through the crowd, his bells jingling as he made jokes. Anyone who couldn't answer his riddles was dragged away, placed in the stocks and wet rag balls hurled at them, much to the crowd's delight.

All too soon, it was time to make their way back to the wagons for the journey home and as they took their places the Reverend. Barclay came over to join the trio.

"Have you enjoyed the day?" he asked.

"You bet," said Jake tightly holding a box of cakes to eat on the journey home.

"He means, yes and thank you for asking us," said Mike, realising the Reverend was a little confused by Jake's reply. Mike then handed around a big bag of humbugs for everyone to enjoy.

A while later, the vicar, who was sitting next Beth, said quietly. "I will ask around about the sweep's boy and see if I can find out about his family. The sweep and his boy have moved on to Torrington and will not be back in our area for a while."

They were all tired by the time they arrived back at Wattle Peak. Once there Beth noticed that the front garden had been tidied up and looked quite nice. All, as usual, was quiet.

They wearily climbed the stairs into the attic and opened the trunk, pleased when their own attic came into view. Changing quickly, they headed back down stairs. It had been a wonderful day and as they walked back home they talked about the things each enjoyed the most. Beth wondered what the vicar would find out about the sweep's boy.

---

# Chapter 8

## New Tenants

It was a lovely day in May as they put on their costumes and opened the trunk. The room whirled, as they were surrounded by sparkles. When all was still once more, the children made their way down the stairs into the tack room for their fifth visit, as Jake asked them, “What’s black and yellow and very dangerous?”

“I don’t know, what is black and yellow and dangerous?” replied Mike, used to Jake’s jokes.

“Shark infested custard,” he replied. Beth and Mike were laughing as they had not heard that daft joke before. They emerged from the tack room into Victorian times once again. They stopped dead in their tracks, on seeing a young lad of about ten years old, standing hands on hips, watching them. On his head he had a peaked cap and he was dressed in a smart dark blue suit with a square white collar edged with blue stripes round it.

“Pray, who are you and why were you in our farmhouse attic? You are trespassing,” he said sternly.

“Were we?” said Beth smiling, “we did not intend to, we were just looking for our dog, Sooty. He ran in through the open gate into your grounds and as the farmhouse door was open, we thought he had gone inside and we went in, to see if we could find him."

"A likely story, you can tell that to the judge," the boy replied scowling.

"Who is it, Lewis?" an elderly man's voice rang out. "What is going on?"

As they moved on to the front drive, they saw an elderly man with a rug over his legs sitting in a wicker chair. The chair had three wheels and was called a bath-chair. He had obviously been enjoying the sunshine. "Please, come on over," he called in a loud voice. He had grey curly hair, long sideburns and glasses perched on the end of his nose. His face was lit up by a big smile. They returned his smile and joined him by the front door where, nearby, a bench had been added to the front garden. "Let me apologise for Lewis's hasty comments. He spends too much time on his own and needs to learn some social manners." Just then, Sooty poked his head out from behind Beth's dress and walked over to the old man, before standing on his hind legs and resting his paws on the old man's knees.

"What a lovely dog," said the man, rubbing his fingers over Sooty's head, as the dog's tail wagged in delight.

"I do apologise for our intrusion," said Mike. "Our dog Sooty had belonged to the previous owners of Wattle Peak and had scampered in, when he saw the gate open." Mike turned and introduced his brother and sister to the elderly man.

"I'm pleased to meet you all; we only moved in about two weeks ago. Today's mild weather has made it a pleasure to sit here. Luckily for me, the caretaker tidied up the front garden, when he knew we were coming but I'm afraid the back garden is in a terrible a mess. The builders will be in soon to decorate parts of the house. Hopefully the weather will hold.

"My son owns the house, but is away until maybe next year. My grandson Lewis and I are on our own at present, apart from our housekeeper-come-cook Mrs Jenkins, a real treasure and my man servant, Wilkins, who is on an errand at present. Do have a seat young lady," and he patted the bench next to him.

"We are pleased to meet you." said Beth, as she sat down.

"I'm Joseph Mandeville, by the way, retired now from my businesses in Exeter," he said, shaking her hand. "That young man is my grandson, Lewis."

Beth could see the boy was a little wary of the dog and called Sooty to her and told him to sit. "Come and say hello to Sooty," she said, encouragingly to Lewis, "he will not harm you, I promise." Lewis slowly approached.

"Open your hand out flat," said Mike, "that way a dog knows you mean it no harm." Sooty licked the boy's hand and sat down in front of him. Lewis gingerly put his hand on the soft fur of the dog's head and his eyes lit up, as he smiled.

"That's right," said Jake reassuringly, "now tickle him behind his ears and he will be your friend for life." Soon Lewis was laughing, as Sooty rolled over, waiting for him to tickle his tummy.

"He loves his tummy tickled too," explained Beth.

"We know the house quite well," she continued, "and it's nice to see it being used again."

"Has your cook settled in alright?" asked Jake. "I could show her where everything is, a previous cook was a good friend, she even let me make some fruit buns."

"Do you want to be a chef, young man? The best cooks are said to be men and are much sought after by the big houses and even by royalty."

"I'm not sure what I want to do yet, but it is a thought."

"Well as you know where the kitchen is and Wilkins is not here at present would you be kind enough to ask cook if we could have tea in the drawing room. You will join us, won't you?" to which the trio nodded and Jake made a dash for the kitchen.

***

After tea and biscuits, Beth asked if she could see the garden. "Please, do take a look. Lewis, why don't you go with Beth?" suggested the old gentleman. Once Lewis was out of the way, Mr Mandeville asked the boys if they knew of any children of about Lewis's age who could come and play with him.

"No, but perhaps the Reverend Barclay might," said Mike, "next time I see him, I will ask him and maybe Lewis could come out with us some time?"

"Thank you that would be kind of you.

"It's just that I don't want him cooped up here with just me all the time. His sisters are much older and are away with their parents."

***

"The garden will need someone with a scythe to cut the grass," said Beth, returning from her tour of the back garden. The hand mower she'd seen wouldn't be able to cope with grass that long.

"Wilkins and I spent many happy hours gardening at my last house," replied Mr Mandeville, "that is, until I became ill, it's such a pity that I can no longer stand for long."

"The garden seems shorter than I remember," commented Beth.

"Yes, my son sold off some of the rear end. It was far too big for us and it did not appear to have been looked after very well. It had been left to go wild."

"Well, luckily, the bit he sold didn't include the greenhouse. That stands at the far end of your current garden," replied Beth, "you could work at the bench there, potting and doing cuttings or work on a tray across your chair. Once the grass has been cut, it would be easy for Wilkins to push you to it.

You might want to think about having a conservatory, then if the staging is built at the right height, your chair could fit under it, allowing you to work there and grow exotic plants, such as orchids, cacti and even oranges.

"What a good idea" he replied, with a grateful smile.

"We were thinking of going down on to the beach for a while. Would you like us to take Lewis with us?" asked Mike, "we will take care of him, on the steps down."

"You have had no lunch. Why don't I ask cook to rustle up a small hamper for you all. Jake, would you see cook for me please and make the arrangements?" said the old gentleman looking tired, "and ask Mrs Jenkins to serve my lunch in here. I shall be glad of a nap, while Lewis is out with you."

Half an hour later, they set off down the cliff path to the beach. Mike kept Lewis on the inside by the cliff face, while Beth had Sooty on his lead and Jake followed up behind with the hamper.

The old jetty was still in good repair and a small sailing boat was tied up there.

"Does the boat belong to Wattle Peak?" asked Mike.

"Yes, I believe grandfather is going to have it checked out, to see if it is still seaworthy," replied Lewis. They chose to sit there to have their lunch.

“Do you know any of the history of this bay, Lewis?” asked Mike. The young boy shook his head. “Well then,” said Mike, “let me tell you, that a time long ago there were smugglers using the caves here,” While they sat munching their lunch, Mike told the tale of the smugglers, the battle that took place there and how they were eventually captured on the beach by a Captain Watson. Lewis sat enthralled, as the story was told. Mike left out their own part, in helping to capture the villains, back in Georgian times.

When the tide had gone out they spent their time playing ball with Sooty on the beach and collecting shells.

“I think it’s time we went back to your grandfather,” said Beth, with a yawn. “It’s a long climb up,” she warned Lewis when he pleaded to stay a while longer.

Jake took out his watch, “Its five o’clock, won’t cook be starting your supper soon? Your grandfather doesn’t like to eat late or so cook told me.”

“Yes, that’s true,” said Lewis reluctantly, “but can we do this again sometime?

“Maybe,” said Mike.

They were all worn out by the time they reached the top and as they reached the grounds of Wattle Peak, Mr Mandeville was pleased to see Lewis safe and sound. Lewis was bursting to tell him of the sights he’d seen and the story of the smugglers.

“Will you not stay for supper?” asked the old gentleman eagerly, pleased to see his grandson so happy.

"No thank you, sir," replied Mike, "we are expected back and have to walk down to near Torrington."

"When will you be this way again?" he asked, "maybe then you could stay for dinner."

"We are not sure when we shall next be here, but we would be pleased to take you up on your offer, at a later date," replied Beth.

They said their goodbyes in the dining room and left by the side gate as usual, returning shortly after to make their way home via the attic once more.

They chatted happily while walking home, pleased to have made new friends to visit. They were also looking forward to the birthday party, in a few weeks' time, when the twins would be 14 years old. "I must remember to take them some of your birthday cake on our next trip. There is always plenty to spare," said Jake and the others agreed it was a good idea.

---

## Chapter 9

### Birthday Party

The twin's birthday party was to be a grand celebration and was being held in the garden. Many of the parents of their friends were also invited so it became quite a big affair. Their mother had made two birthday cakes. One in the shape of a cricket bat for Mike and the other in the shape of a record, on which she had included the name 'Adam Ant', Beth's favourite pop star. The red balloons were a great favourite, as within each was the number of the goody bag you were to take home, as even fourteen year olds were not too old to enjoy sweets and the fun of popping the balloons.

"Come on," said Beth, to her best friend Sara and her other girlfriends, "I'll show you the items held in the Victorian trunk." The boys and their friends made their way down to the beach, leaving the parents and other friends to sit in the garden in the glorious sunshine.

The laughter, coming from the farmhouse attic, could be heard by Beth's mother while in the kitchen. When the girls left the attic, they came through to the kitchen and Beth's mother asked them what all the laughter had been about in the attic.

"Oh, Beth put on the red Victorian outfit for us to see and then bent over, showing us the awful pantaloons they wore in

Victorian times," Sara explained, with a giggle. "Beth also showed us how difficult it was to sit on a modern chair in a crinoline and just how careful you had to be in case you flashed your underwear and shocked the vicar."

"Mind you," said Beth's Mother with a little laugh, "some of the miniskirts I have seen around leave little to the imagination. Think of the scandal they'd have caused back in Victorian times. Did you know, girls," she whispered, "it was not so many years before those pantaloons became fashionable that they didn't wear any underwear at all," to which the girls squealed loudly at the thought. "So maybe, the pantaloons weren't so awful after all," laughed Mary.

The girls still said they were glad they did not have to wear them, even if, as Beth had explained, it had become fashionable for a while to show off the bottom edges with fancy lace added.

"I liked the Victorian summer dress best." said Sara.

"Oh no, the wine dress worn in winter was far the better of the two," said another of her friends.

"I haven't seen them yet," said Beth's mother, intrigued.

As the afternoon wore on, a tape deck was plugged in and the dancing began. The children laughed, as their parents tried to copy their dance moves.

Jake quietly returned to the kitchen and wrapped some cake in cling film before placing it in a tin, as a present for the Mandevilles.

## Chapter 10

### The Decorators

The room swirled, as they arrived back in Victorian times, for their sixth visit. “Oh no,” cried Beth, as she poked her head into the main room and saw two straw pallets with blankets on the floor. Two tin mugs stood close by and some clothes were seen hung on the wall pegs, “Someone is using the room!”

“Now what do we do?” said Mike.

“I’m not sure, but thank goodness we hid the trunk in the other room, even if there is only just enough space to get past it,” replied Beth, “after all; the last thing we want is someone fooling about with it.”

“It might be wiser not to visit today. It could be dangerous if we can’t get back into the attic. What did the diary indicate?” asked Mike.

“Only that the decorators were to be paid for three weeks work, so they should have been finished a few days ago,” she replied looking puzzled.

“It’ll be okay,” said Jake, optimistically, “they will be busy working in the main house most of the day, so we will just have to make it a short visit. After all, we don’t want to waste the trip do we?”

“Hmm… okay then,” said Mike reluctantly

Cautiously, Mike made his way downstairs to see what was happening. Moments later he was back and telling them there was a lot of equipment, ladders and the like in the tack room.

"Maybe, they have nearly finished their work then," said Beth.

"Okay, let's go and see what we can find out," replied Mike, taking charge for once. "I'll go first, Beth you go last and be ready at a moment's notice to dive back up to the attic and into the narrow room, if needs be."

Once safely out onto the drive, they saw Mr Mandeville and another man, whose hair was silver and brown, his eyebrows quite bushy.

"Hello there," called the old gentleman, as they approached. "Wilkins, come and meet my new friends," and he introduced the children to his manservant, a man nearly as old as himself. Shall we have tea here today?"

"Yes please," said Jake.

"Would you arrange that, please, Wilkins," instructed Mr Mandeville, "and bring out a few extra chairs."

"Let me see cook for you, Wilkins, I need to talk to her" said Jake.

"Thank you young sir, I'll get the chairs," and off they both went.

Beth seated herself on a chair, where she found it much easier to arrange her dress, rather than on the bench where her skirt would have taken up most of the room.

***

Jake had brought enough birthday cake with him for them all, including cook. He liked Mrs Jenkins, a plump lady, her auburn hair shot through with silver. She had told him on their previous visit about some of her family. She had no home of her own, so was unable to have her old father live with her. When he had become too old and weak to work, he had gone into the workhouse.

"How is your father?" asked Jake.

"Oh, I have been to visit him since we last met," said Mrs Jenkins, putting the large kettle on the range to heat up. "I hated seeing him in there. It's an awful place where things have gone from bad to worse in recent years." She reached up to the shelf to get down all the crockery necessary and Jake arranged these for her on the large tray.

"I wasn't even allowed to see him on his own," she said, near to tears. "He told me the food was dreadful and left him hungry. He said all the men at mealtimes had to sit in long lines facing the front and were not allowed to speak, so it was a miserable time. He sits all day in a room with other infirm men. Even the able-bodied inmates are no longer allowed to go out and about, so have no chance to look for work or to get out of that dreadful place for good. If you leave, you are not allowed ever, to go back."

“I always thought those places were there to help the poor,” remarked Jake.

“At one time people could avoid such places when there was a shortage of work, thanks to the parish paying ‘out door relief’ to help tide them over, as most work was seasonal. This meant you could stay together with your family in your own home and once the work started up again, you no longer needed the parish’s help. Such help is a thing of the past now, the parish councils declared it too expensive a system to continue. Unfortunately, at the same time they made the conditions in the workhouse harder, to discourage the poor from going there.”

She wiped away a tear or two with her apron, as she told Jake about the small children in those places, separated from their parents, except for an hour or so on Sundays. Her father was lucky, for she had always taken him some food, as Mr Mandeville was a very generous man.

“I had better make more tea, as those two lazy decorators will want theirs and I would rather they did not come into my kitchen. You need eyes in the back of your head, with them around. They should have finished the work days ago and left with the rest of the workmen, but claimed further work was needed. I can’t see that they have done anything more to the main bedroom. It looked finished to me. I think they know they are on to a good thing, if you ask me, as they are well-fed and paid for doing nothing. They will be demanding their lunch at 1pm and their dinner at 6pm, plus they even have accommodation over in the farmhouse attic if you please!" said cook indignantly.

"I don't like the sound of them," said Jake, "tell them the attic is haunted by ghosts," he said, with a twinkle in his eye. "That might shift them. Just then the door opened, as Wilkins arrived to collect the tray.

When Jake returned to the others where the wooden stand for the tea tray had already been set up. Jake carried the birthday cake on a plate while Wilkins carried the heavily laden tray. Everyone enjoyed the cake. Jake had left the cake tin in the kitchen and the cling-film was carefully hidden in his pocket. They all wished the twins a belated happy birthday.

***

"Where is Sooty?" said Lewis.

"Sorry Lewis, we left him at home to keep our Mother company," explained Beth. When she saw how disappointed he was she squeezed his hand, "Don't worry, we will bring him next time and you may hold his lead."

"Oh, may I?" and his face lit up as Beth nodded her head smiling at him. She felt sorry for the lad having no playmates.

"Have the decorators been here ever since our last visit?" asked Mike, keen to know what was going on.

"Just about, I understand they are almost finished, just a little more work needed to the main bedroom apparently," replied Mr Mandeville, at this comment. Mike noticed Wilkins raised an eyebrow.

"May we take Lewis with us to the church?" Beth asked, as she turned to Mr Mandeville. "It is a nice walk." She was eager to see the Reverend Barclay once more.

"Why not?" he replied.

It was a fine day. As they walked along Beth held Lewis's hand and told him the story of Highwayman Joe and his grisly end, so it didn't seem long before the church came into view.

"We'll take Lewis to have a look around the graveyard, while you look for the vicar," said Mike and the boys hurried off. Beth waved as they left her and she made for the vicarage. Luckily the vicar had just returned home and was pleased to see her.

"Come into the garden, Beth, it's too nice to stay indoors. Where are your brothers?"

"Oh, they will be over shortly, they are just showing Lewis Mandeville around the church and graveyard. Lewis's father is the owner of the houses at Wattle Peak. I will introduce him to you in a little while. His grandfather is staying with him and the rest of their family will join them later this year or early next."

"The Mandevilles you say. I must make a point of visiting them sometime soon."

"One of my reasons for visiting you today was a promise we made to Lewis's grandfather, namely to ask your help in finding someone suitable for Lewis to play with and maybe even to study together. His grandfather doesn't want the lad, now ten years old, to be lonely."

"I see. Well, leave it with me and I'll give it some thought. Now, I have some news for you about that little boy, Simon."

"Simon?"

"The sweep's boy."

"Oh, what have you found out?" asked Beth.

"His mother, Mrs Jamison and the rest of the family were living just outside Pennington, on the road leading up to the highway. It's the one we took to St Ives."

"Yes, I remember."

"It was only a shack. I managed to speak to a few of her friends. It seems that Mrs. Jamison's husband died in a mining accident. She was then pregnant with twins and already had three other children, Lisa ten, Barry nine, plus Simon who was then just eight years old. She was a good needle woman and trained Lisa to help her sew shirts. However, soon after her husband died, the amount she was paid went down, so that she was only making one and a half pence per shirt. She was barely able to feed her growing family, who often went hungry. She heard there was better money to be made at the potteries near Hayle, where they would also employ not only her, but the younger children as well, as there are no 'industrial acts' applying to the potteries."

"But what about her babies, who would take care of them, whilst she was working?"

"That was the problem. She decided, when the twins were three months old, to place them full time with a Mrs Wicken, a babyminder, but needed to pay her two months in advance. As a result, she went to Grimshaw, the sweep. He'd been pestering her to sell Simon to him, as he was small for an eight year old. She needed the money and knew it would only be for a couple of years, until Simon would be too large for the work and the sweep would have to let him go. Until then, the sweep would have to feed and clothe him. Mr Grimshaw told her he would look after the boy.

"I know she must have been desperate," said Beth, trying to understand her actions.

"Yes, believe me, she was. Mrs Jamison hoped that when Simon returns to them he, too, would work at the potteries. By that time, both Lisa and Barry would be grown up enough to earn better money and with the additional wages Simon would earn, they would then be in a position to have the babies back. They would work in shifts, so they could look after the little ones between them and would be a united family once more."

"Wasn't what she did like selling Simon into slavery?" whispered Beth, a look of horror on her face.

"I'm afraid so but she had very little choice and I seriously doubt the potteries are a good place to work. I have heard that many workers die at an early age there, just like the chimney sweep boys, as the fine dust gets into their lungs."

“Isn’t that what they call a case of out of the frying pan into the fire?” said Beth

“Just so,” said the vicar nodding. “There is worse yet, I’m afraid. I had a woman come to see me last week, in despair about her children, who were with the same baby minder, that Wicken woman. She missed her children very much and wanted to see them more often than just on the day she paid the fees. But was not allowed in when she called on another day. So when the maid went to get wood from the shed, it gave her an opportunity to creep inside the house. Her children were not in the room she normally saw them in, during the short 30 minute visit allowed each month. She made her way up the stairs, looking for them and was appalled at the number of children there. She saw at one side of the room, empty gin and laudanum bottles and knew then, why they were so unusually quiet. Mrs Wicken had drugged them to keep them quiet. They were not being properly looked after. Many were suffering from malnutrition.

“That’s terrible,” said Beth, close to tears.

“I’m afraid so. I had heard rumours that she sells some babies to childless couples, if the mothers owe more than three months fees. She claims the parents have abandoned the child. The struggling mothers when they do turn up having somehow scraped together the money are distraught as they have no chance of getting their babies back. They mostly can’t read and do not realise that they could be giving up their rights when they sign the agreement. Some maintain they did not owe Mrs Wicken any money but she sold their children anyway.

Where the parents owe her money for older children, then once they reach five years old I suspect she sells them to the owners of small trades, like the undertakers, shoe makers and such. Perhaps you have read, 'Oliver Twist' so you know what sort of a life they led."

"Yes, I have," replied Beth, "unfortunately."

"I'm sorry to shock you, Beth, but that is the way of life for the poor. There are girls of your age who would have been married for almost two years and have babies of their own. Amongst the poor, you would be expected to be one of the bread winners and deal with such problems."

"I know you are right, but it's a dreadful way of life for so many."

"One does what one can to help," he continued, "but it does no good to dwell on it," he sighed. "Tea and sandwiches, I think," he said, changing the subject. "Here come the others, so I will go and see cook," and with that he disappeared inside. Beth decided to tell her brothers about Simon's sad tale, later on.

***

They started back soon after lunch. Once at the main house Mike went and spoke to Wilkins about what cook had told Jake regarding the decorators. Wilkins confirmed that he suspected she was right, but he did not want to distress his master about the matter.

Mike wheeled the elderly Mr Mandeville in his bath-chair through to the drawing room, an easy job as he was quite slim and quite light. Mike placed the chair close to the fire and made sure it was in the correct position. "Mr Mandeville, may I go and see the rooms that have been decorated?"

"Please do," he replied, "I have not been able to see the upstairs rooms for myself and would be interested to know what you think."

Mike quietly moved up the stairs and stood in the room next to the one the decorators were working in. He could hear the men chatting. One of them was leaning against the open window frame, so Mike could hear them plainly.

"This is a sweet number," said one, "how long do you think we can keep it going?"

"Another week perhaps. Any longer than that we might find the boss coming to check up on us," the other replied with a chuckle.

"We could always spend the rest of the afternoon at the King's Head, in the village. Grab a couple of empty paint cans. We'll claim we needed to get more paint from the hardware store."

As soon as the men disappeared from the house Mike went into the room where they were supposed to be decorating. He checked the brushes, none of which were wet after cleaning or had been placed in turps, to soak. The walls and woodwork weren't wet or even tacky, so he knew no work had been done there that day. The job appeared to have been completed.

"The rooms looked fine and that a good job had been done," Mike told Mr Mandeville on his return.

When Mike saw Wilkins again, he confirmed he was right. They agreed not to say anything to the old gentleman about the men. "I think I know of a way to get them out," said Mike.

As the trio said goodbye to the Mandevilles, they were able to see the decorators in the distance, as they made their way back along the cliff top road. Beth and the boys left by the side gate and then re-entered unseen, a few minutes later. Mike disappeared into the stables before he followed the other two into the tack room. He was carrying a large tin cup and several large white dust sheets that had been used to cover up the furniture in the main house, while it had no tenant, plus a few other things. Beth and Jake were puzzled as to what Mike was up to as he'd pushed them ahead of him, up the stairs, telling them to hurry. Once in the attic he explained what they would have to do.

A short while later the sun was setting. All three children were in the narrow room and seated on the trunk, careful to make no noise. They heard the two men, as they came stumbling up the stairs laughing, clearly they had been drinking.

As the men flopped onto their pallets, still joking, they heard a noise like a soft moan, at which the smaller man, known as little Johnny, looked over with a worried frown at his mate Fred, The room was in semi darkness, and they heard another moan, louder this time, and a rattle of chains, coming closer. The two men, wide eyed, jumped to their feet; little Johnny pushed Fred towards the door, "Go see what it is," he said, his voice quaking, as his hands shook too much to light a candle.

The door then began to creak as it opened. A terrified Fred took a step back, knocking into his mate. They continued to back away, as a small, deathly white apparition with jangling chains, moved slowly towards them, its hair white and its eyes so piercing, they seemed to shine out of its ashen face, like beacons. The white, ghostly figure was followed by a taller, white shapeless form, as the moaning started again. With a terrified cry, the two men headed for the stairs, with the apparitions slowly following them. The two workmen disappeared down the stairs, falling over each other, in their rush to get out of the tack room door.

"Cook told us there was a ghost, but I never believed her," said Fred, as they stood outside shaking. On seeing the men, Wilkins walked over to them.

"What's up with you two?" he asked.

"Didn't you hear it?" asked Fred, with a shiver, "the moaning and clanking of chains, you must have heard them, man!"

"No, I heard nothing and it's obvious you both have been drinking," replied Wilkins.

"It must have been a trick," said little Johnny and he persuaded Wilkins to go up with him to the attic. There was nothing in the main room and after gingerly opening the door of the narrow room, he found nothing in there, having checked every nook and cranny.

Now even more shaken, Johnny went back down stairs, vowing never to go in there again!

"There is nowhere else for you to sleep," said Wilkins, "and the master will hear of your drinking. You two are a disgrace."

The men decided to sleep in the cold stables for the night and they told Wilkins they would be off in the morning, leaving someone else to collect the equipment.

Back in 1982 once more, Beth and her brothers laughed, as Mike and Jake took off their sheets. Jake, who had worn his sheet poncho-like, having made a hole in the centre, stood busily shaking his head over the sheet, trying to get the plaster powder off his face and hair. Mike had poured a mug full of the stuff over Jake's head, and ash from the decorator's ashtray, had been used to darken the area around Jake's eyes, to make them stand out. The latter had been Beth's idea, something she learnt at her drama class, but now poor Jake needed to get cleaned up, before he changed back into his own clothes.

"I hope the plaster does not set, when you get in the shower Jake," said Beth, laughing at the thought. Her part in the deed had been to moan like a ghost and to clear up all traces of the plaster dust. "Let's hope it's done the trick and those two crooks have decided to leave." Beth took pity on Jake and got out a hair brush and helped to clean his hair, leaving Mike to put the chains and old sheets by the trunk, ready to take back to the stables on their next visit to the past.

Beth suddenly remembered she hadn't told them about her talk with the vicar, regarding Simon and his family. She decided to leave it until the next day, rather than spoil an evening that had ended so well.

Just before they entered their home, Mike told them that Mr Mandeville suggested they might like to accompany him and Lewis on a visit to Redruth, where he had an appointment with his old friend and solicitor.

"I did explain," said Mike, "that I was not sure we would be able to take up his kind offer. Mr Mandeville assured me that as long we arrived at Wattle Peak by 9.30 am on the 21st July the offer remained open and he hoped we would be able to join him as he has a treat in store for us all."

---

## Chapter 11

### Summer

At long last the school holidays had arrived, six whole weeks - more time than they knew what to do with. School had finished early on the last day, so Beth, Mike and Jake were lazing around in the garden, enjoying hot and sunny weather. The garden was looking its best. Their mother had been busy putting in bedding plants, whilst halfway down the garden, their father had placed a trellis fence, so he could start a vegetable bed behind it. He said he hoped to keep Sooty out of the area, knowing he would be tempted to bury his bones there, instead of in his wife's flower beds.

Beth told her brothers what she had learned about Simon and his family, as she handed out the glasses of lemonade her mother had left on the table. They wondered what they could do, to help the poor sweep's boy.

"We don't even know if he is back in the area," said Mike.

"We might ask the vicar to let us know, via his housekeeper, who is friendly with cook," suggested Jake, as he rolled over on the lawn, shielding his eyes with his hand from the sun, as he looked up at Beth.

"A good idea," Beth replied as she sat down on the lawn.

“I think there is something we maybe could do to help him but I need to check a few facts first,” said Mike thoughtfully.

“If we are going with Mr Mandeville to Redruth, in two days’ time,” continued Beth, as she brushed off the bits of grass clinging to her the skirt, “I think I should get our summer Victorian clothes ready, as we shall want to look our best.” With that she got up and disappeared to the attic.

Beth sorted through the trunk, until she found the boys light-weight jackets and trousers. The jackets were blue and the trousers light grey. Their waistcoats were grey with a blue fleck and there were neck scarves of pale grey silk, to wear with their white, fine cotton, collarless shirts.

Beth lifted out a pretty pink and cream summer dress. The skirt had several tiers, each tier was edged with dark pink satin ribbon. The material, soft muslin, was much lighter than she had worn before. It was very suitable for warm days, one had a small floral printed design. The sleeves were wide at the top and narrow from half way down the forearm to the wrist. The neck was square. The bodice was looser than that of the winter dress for which Beth was grateful, as otherwise she would have found the dress very warm, with its long sleeves. Thinking about it, she realised she hadn’t seen any Victorian women wearing short sleeve dresses during the day. She found a pretty sun brolly, in pink and cream, with a frill all around its rim.

She had just lifted out some cream satin pumps, when she heard her mother calling up the stairs. "Are you there Beth?"

"Yes mum."

"Oh good," said her mother, as she reached the top step, camera in hand. "The boys said you were looking through the Victorian trunk and after what your friends at the party said about its clothes, I wanted to see them for myself. A picture of you in one of the outfits would be nice."

Seeing the pink dress lying over the chair, she lifted it up, "Now, this is lovely," said her mother, "why not put it on for me and I wouldn't mind seeing the wine coloured winter outfit as well?"

"The winter outfit would look great on you, mum, why don't you try it on? We're much the same size now," said Beth, quite excited.

"Okay, I will," replied her mother, with a laugh, "it would be fun."

There was much giggling to be heard as they helped each other to dress.

Beth clipped the false hair pieces; two bunches of ringlets, to her mother's hair, as the finishing touch, just as her father came up the stairs. "Look at you two," he said, "don't you look wonderful. I heard all the laughter when I was putting the car away."

"I'm glad you're here. Would you take our picture?" asked Beth, as she made her way to the window sill to get the camera and hand it to him.

“Right, stand against that wall together. Could you both move over to the left the light is better there?” They shuffled over a bit, “that’s better, say cheese.” He also took pictures of each of them, on their own.

“Your turn dad,” said Beth and brought out the top hat that Mike wore and his light weight blue jacket, which was slightly tight on her father. She wound the cravat around his neck, to hide his shirt, but noted that the trousers were too short for him, so she sat him in a chair with the jacket done up and stood her mother slightly behind him. “Something is missing,” said Beth puzzled, “I know,” and returned with a walking stick. She stood it on the floor in front of him and placed both his hands on the top of the cane to hold it there. Satisfied, Beth said “Oh yes, that will make a fine portrait,” and lined up her picture to show her father from the waist up. “Breathe in dad and smile, both of you,” and quickly clicked the camera button. ‘What a handsome Victorian couple they would have made, ’thought Beth.

After spending some time discussing the things in the trunk, Beth and her mother went into the narrow room to change out of their costumes. When they returned, Beth found her father browsing the pages of the Victorian newspaper, “I must come up and read this another day,” he said, before carefully putting it back in the trunk.

As it was not part of the contents of Uncle Sedgwick’s trunk, it wasn’t covered by the terms of the Will. Beth was tempted to suggest to her father that he took it home to read, but realised it might give rise to too many questions and thought better of it.

"Yes, that's a good idea," said Beth, "you'll find it ever so interesting." As she saw her parents about to descend the stairs, she called to them "I'll be with you shortly, when I've tidied up in here."

Beth heard her parents talking, as they left the attic, "Looks like they really are taking care of the items in those trunks," remarked her mother.

"You're right, Mary, but then didn't we always know they were sensible kids," stated her father.

Beth followed them, some ten minutes later. Her thoughts were on her next visit, wondering what Mr Mandeville's surprise would be and wishing she had had such a grandfather, never having known her own.

---

# Chapter 12

## Redruth

Two days later they arrived back in time at 9.15am and they were dressed in their summer clothes. The boys had their top hats with them. Beth wore a straw bonnet, plus a cream shawl, as they made their way up to the Georgian House, where they saw a large carriage and horses waiting. When they entered the drawing room, Mr Mandeville explained he had hired the rig from the King's Head for their trip. Lewis beamed excitedly as he saw them arrive.

"We are pleased you have decided to come. Don't you all look smart and Beth, you look so pretty in pink."

"Thank you," replied Beth with a blush.

"Right, now it's time we got settled in the coach," said Mr Mandeville. "Mike, I have a favour to ask. Would you be willing to push my bath-chair today so I may give Wilkins the day off?"

"Yes, of course, no problem at all."

"I could help too," said Jake, not to be outdone.

"Maybe," replied Mr Mandeville, smiling broadly. "Come along everyone, let's make our way to the carriage."

"Where's Sooty?" asked Lewis, looking around.

"We'll bring him next time," said Beth, putting her arm through his, as they walked to the carriage, which looked quite grand with its black gleaming paintwork and its brass fittings, sparkling in the sunlight. There were two carriage lamps at the front, just in case it should be dark when they travelled home. They patted the two shiny black horses before climbing into the carriage, which was a closed-in compartment with soft leather seats plus sash windows, so useful on such a warm day. The five of them were soon settled in, with Lewis and Beth on one side and the others sitting opposite. The driver had secured the bath-chair onto the roof and with a "Giddy up" they were off and up into Pennington, soon passing the King's Head, then out of the Square, up towards the main highway. The countryside was bright green, as the trees were in full leaf and a slightly damp smell was noticeable as it had rained earlier. As they looked down the hillside, large flocks of birds, like small dark clouds were seen wheeling over the fields before they swooped, landing where the wheat had been cut.

After a while, Mike spotted that they had just passed the signpost to Hayle and thought this strange, as they appeared to be heading north rather than east.

"Mr Mandeville, are we going the right way, we seem to be on the road to Hayle?" enquired Mike puzzled.

"I was hoping you wouldn't have noticed but I'll say no more for now, I don't want to spoil the surprise," he said, with a wink.

Soon they entered Hayle and the carriage turned up the main High Street, then through a busy road where carts and hansom cabs stood. Boxes were piled high along the pavement as men were busy loading these on to trolleys.

"Here we are, everybody out," said Mr Mandeville, with a chuckle.

"It's a train station," cried the youngsters excitedly.

"Yes and we have tickets booked for the 10.45am. train but have only 10 minutes, so don't wander off. I'll go with Mike to collect them and meet you on the platform shortly."

The coachman brought the bath-chair to the station entrance, as Mr Mandeville held on to Mike's arm and walked slowly to the ticket office to pick up their first class tickets. He had booked the whole carriage, hoping they would be coming on the trip. The bath-chair was carried by the porter to the train carriage and was once more stowed away.

Mike helped the old gentleman into the wooden carriage with its comfortable seats of plush red velvet, the compartment very much resembling the coach they had just left, only larger. There were three individual first class compartments joined together. Each compartment held eight persons and although joined together they had no corridors. They found the first class compartment, reserved just for them. There were two similar, but smaller, second class carriages, each of three compartments. These had smaller windows and lightly padded seats. Behind these, were three third class carriages with only a roof and sides that reached half way up but no windows. In these, the unfortunate passengers sat either on wooden benches or stood up, if full. Flat-bed trucks followed at the rear with goods tied on and covered with tarpaulin. The carriages were painted cream and brown with large initials W. C. R. painted in gold, these standing for 'West Cornwall Railway.'

Mike soon found the others, where they stood admiring the steam engine. Smoke was gently puffing out of its tall chimney at the front. The stoker was busily placing a few shovels of coal in the boiler. The green and gold paint of the engine shone in the sunshine. There was a rounded tall brass dome in the centre, standing proud of the long cylinder body that covered the engine.

"What's that for?" asked Jake, after the engineer had finished explaining how the boiler heated the water, which created the steam that moved the pistons, which in turn spun the wheels.

"That brass dome is where the safety valve is kept. If too much steam builds up, it goes in there to prevent it blowing up and we would not want that would we?" he told them gravely.

"Nearly time to go now," said the flag carrying porter, when he saw they still hadn't taken their seats.

"Would you like to toot the horn, young man?" asked the engine driver, turning to Lewis.

"Oh, yes please," replied Lewis, eyes wide with surprise. Mike then helped Lewis up on to the footplate and the engine driver lifted him up.

"Pull the cord twice, only to let people know we are almost ready to leave and then hurry off to your carriage," instructed the driver. Two piercing ‘toots’ were heard. Then a grinning Lewis hurried back along the platform with the boys and Beth, towards the open carriage door. Soon they were all seated and the whistle was blown by the station master, as the porter waved his flag.

At first the train moved slowly as it got up steam and soon it had left the station far behind and the clackerty-clack of the wheels were heard as the speed mounted and smoke started to invade the compartment. Mike swiftly closed the window, when Mr Mandeville began coughing. “That’s better,” said Mr Mandeville, gratefully.

Beth noted how much more room there was in the train compartment, than there had been in the coach. They crowded around the windows to see the small farms and fields with hedges all around, a patchwork of various colours of greens, yellows and reds, according to the crops. They passed by meadows, some with sheep, others with cows or horses. There were little hamlets of four or five houses with thatched or slate roofs and assorted sized barns, plus large wooded areas.

“We’re travelling quite a bit faster than the coach,” stated Mike.

“So how fast are we travelling?” asked Jake, as he turned to Mr Mandeville.

“Oh, I’d say on average about 30 miles an hour, whereas the coach we were on earlier, did about 7 miles. This is nothing compared to the Great Western Railway, on which I travelled last year. On the route from Paddington to Bristol we moved at over 60 miles per hour, that was really something," said Mr Mandeville, smiling at the memory. "I had to change trains once more at Truro for the rest of my journey, as the broad gauge line stops there. I had to move to another platform to board a different train, which uses the same standard gauge track as here. It's only on the broad gauge routes where the tracks have a wider gap between the metal rails that the train can manage the faster speeds. The record stands at 74 miles an hour, can you image that? I wish I had been on board that day," he said, wistfully.

"Gosh, you were lucky, grandfather," said Lewis, sounding envious. "I do wish I was a train driver."

"Much better to own the railway, my boy," his grandfather chuckled.

An hour later, they arrived at Redruth, a lively town, above which hung a granite crag called 'Carn Brea.' Beth saw that the town consisted mainly of grey stone houses, with many shops. She remembered Mr Mandeville had said the town was the centre of the copper industry and boasted the county's largest mine. It was a thriving town, due to the copper needed to make brass, for all kinds of engines. Most of the miners were as poor as ever, only the mine and metal foundry owners, plus their shareholders, had made their fortunes. The owners of the shops, supplying general goods needed by all, were prospering.

They helped Mr Mandeville out of the carriage, while the bath-chair was collected and taken outside. Mike and the old gentleman then made their way slowly to the exit, with the others following.

They realised, as they walked through part of the busy town, that the solicitor's office was on the outskirts, a pleasant ten minute walk away. Soon they found themselves in a tree-lined road, the building they sought, being on its own. It was a three storey house with a large front door painted black and next to it was a shiny brass name plate, stating 'Nicholas Harrison and Rodney Black, Solicitors.'

Mr Mandeville alighted carefully from the bath-chair, as Mike lifted the latch to open the door to help him down the step into the small reception room. At a small desk sat an elderly gentleman, surrounded by books, "Good day to you Joshua," said Mr Mandeville.

"Welcome Sir, we have been expecting you, please go through to the parlour. Mr Harrison is out in the garden. I'll have your chair brought through for you." They made their way down a long corridor, off which there were several rooms and then past a staircase. Here they opened a door onto a large sitting room where a table was laid for lunch. Just then Nicholas Harrison spotted them through the window and came to greet them.

"Good to see you, Joseph," said Mr Harrison, holding out his hand.

"And you, Nicholas," he replied warmly taking his hand.

"I have the documents for you when you are ready. Let me introduce my grandson's new friends, Beth, Mike, and Jake," Mr Harrison then shook the hands of each in turn.

"I'm pleased you all managed to come, there was some doubt that I would have had the pleasure of meeting you today. I'm hoping my sons may join us later; they said they intended to drop in. Let's go out into the garden before we have lunch. It's a shame to waste such a glorious day."

The garden was huge, mainly lawn and it led down to the river, where a few willow trees dipped their leaves in the water. Lewis, who had been there before, disappeared into the kitchen and returned with a large paper bag and proceeded to lead his friends down the garden. "Be back in thirty minutes," called his grandfather who was gratefully sitting once more in his bath-chair with Nicholas seated by his side.

Lewis took the trio on a tour of the garden. As they neared the river, they could see that the water was reddish in colour. Lewis explained that this was due to the residue from the copper ore ending up in the water. Lewis delved into the bag and produced several slices of bread, for feeding the ducks. Soon the ducks were crowding around, quacking loudly and the noise drew two swans from further down the river. These they saw gliding gracefully towards them. The largest swan made its way up the bank, as Jake had shown it the bag, with the remaining bread inside. He laughed, as it followed him around in circles, trying to get at the slices, while he kept the bag's contents just out of its reach. Jake turned to see to if the others were watching and failed to notice the swan lunge at him and squealed as it pecked his bum, causing him to drop the bag. The swan, its wings out-spread chased after Jake, when he tried to retrieve the bread. They all backed away, as Jake rubbed his bottom,

"It's your own fault, bruv, for teasing the swan," said Mike laughing and placed his arm around his brother's shoulder. Jake grinned and the children giggled, as they hurried away from the riverside.

As they walked back to the house they saw Mr Mandeville being wheeled back into the parlour. "There you are, just in time for lunch," exclaimed Mr Harrison, smiling as he ushered them indoors and over to the table with its array of cold food.

Beth smiled. They still had the afternoon to look forward to with Nicholas's sons, who would be dropping by later.

---

## Chapter 13

### Heavens above

After lunch, while Lewis's grandfather was busy signing some papers, the children returned to the garden to consider what game they might play. They were startled by a sudden commotion, as two young men in their late teens, burst out of the parlour door and ran into the back garden, shouting excitedly as they rushed down towards the river. The children followed, wondering what was going on, when a hot air balloon appeared over the tree line heading their way. It seemed vast. The basket hanging below was made of willow and painted yellow, with bags of sand tied around its sides. The huge canopy of the hot air balloon was mainly made up of wide horizontal bands of red, orange and yellow silk.

The children stood and looked on in wonder. Lewis had never seen anything like it before, and wore a worried look until he saw the faces peering down at him from above. "Robbie, Thomas," he called out, where upon the young men in the garden grabbed the rope attached to the balloon's basket that Robbie had thrown down to them and secured it around a small tree before grabbing a second rope and gently guiding the balloon away from the tree and on to the open grass area. The children heard the whoosh of the gas as Thomas kept the balloon inflated as it descended slowly.

"Well, well, well," said Nicholas, hurrying from the parlour, having seen the hot air balloon, "when they said they be would dropping in, I didn't think they meant just that." He laughed on reaching the balloon as his sons climbed out of the high-sided basket and fell to the ground, not having waited for the steps to be put in place. Nicholas hugged them both warmly as they introduced their two friends, Pete and John, from Exeter University, informing those present that the two followed them everywhere by wagon.

Lewis's grandfather knew Nicholas's sons well and shook their hands eagerly. "Come," he said, "and tell us how you came by the balloon?"

The introductions were quickly made and while the grownups sat around the garden table, the children sat on a blanket, close by, not wishing to miss a word of the story.

"Where to start," said Robbie, running his fingers through his hair. "Well, the hot air balloon was a prize in a boxing competition at the local fair." He indicated the lovely black eye sported by his brother. "Of course, they never expected Thomas would win and it was a near thing." Thomas stood up and gave a little bow.

"More fool them," said Nicholas proudly, "I always knew he had the makings of a boxing champion."

"Our friends, Pete and John here, have volunteered to keep an eye on us from the ground and are able to help us land safely as well as securing the balloon, so it doesn't float away. They carry the spare gas supply and transported the folded balloon canopy with its basket, in the wagon, when necessary. There was one occasion when we landed in a haystack, having brushed against a tree first, resulting in us having to do a few repairs. The farmer was none too pleased. He claimed we scared his cows, so we had to deflate the canopy and reassemble it all again elsewhere, to appease him."

"I hope you had a few lessons before first taking it up," said their father somewhat concerned.

"Of course we did," said Thomas.

"Do tell us how it works," said Mr Mandeville.

"Well, first the gas is lit with the air control adjusted to produce a softer yellow flame, to create the warm air, necessary to inflate the silk canopy. It's a flame that will not set fire to it," explained Thomas. "As you may know, warm air rises, as it's much lighter than cold air. You direct the warm air into the canopy until fully inflated and once full you only need to top up the hot air now and again. There's a flap at the top operated by a rope that lets in cold air and the pressure from the heavier cold air helps the balloon to descend. By reducing the amount of hot air going in, it helps us gradually to descend."

Beth sat enthralled, thinking how handsome Thomas was, with his thick black wavy hair. Mike prodded her, "Even better than Adam Ant?" he said in a whisper and Beth felt herself blush, putting her finger to her lip, as Mike grinned.

"Aren't you at the mercy of the wind?" asked Mr Mandeville.

"To some extent we are but by adjusting the weight on the sides of the basket we have some control over direction," Robbie informed them.

"The sandbags of course, that's what they are there for," replied Mr Mandeville, smiling. "If only I were younger and fitter I would be up there with you."

"Would you mind if we visited you next month at Wattle Peak, sir?" asked Thomas seeing how keen he was, "only we will need somewhere to land and to keep the balloon safe, when making our way from the north to the south of Cornwall."

"We would be only too happy to have you, wouldn't we Lewis?" Mr Mandeville replied beaming.

"Will you take us up?" cried the children.

"Well now, we might take you for a ride, but only upwards, the balloon must remain secured here in the garden if Mr Mandeville agrees."

"If you are sure it's safe, then I agree," replied Lewis's grandfather.

"It will be fine, but for today, I think it best we take just the two smaller boys and only Robbie goes with them. You can see the balloon has already begun to lose some of the hot air so the less weight the better, as our gas supply is getting low," explained Thomas.

Mr Mandeville looked at the crestfallen faces of Mike and Beth and promised them there would be another opportunity, when the balloon comes to Wattle Peak and maybe even a flight at the same time.

Robbie mounted the steps this time and climbed into the basket, then reached out to help Jake and Lewis climb in. He pointed out the ridge on the inside, on which they could stand to see over the side. Robbie carefully removed a sandbag from each of the four sides of the basket, to reduce further the weight and opened the valve to let in a noisy burst of hot air to the canopy. Meanwhile, the lads on the ground, carefully played out a length of rope each side, just enough to allow the basket to rise up to about 50 feet. Lewis's and Jake's eyes widened and they grinned as the balloon rose, leaving the ground behind and waved madly at everyone far below. They peered around them, checking how far they could see over hedges and the river. "Look," said Lewis, pointing into the distance, "there's a train. See the smoke and tracks going far into the distance." All too soon, they descended back to earth once more. Both boys babbled on about their short trip to anyone who would listen. They rushed to help with the blocks, needed under one side of the basket, so that the canopy, when deflated, would fall and lie in the direction of the river, clear of any trees or bushes.

"Well, that was very kind of you," said Mr Mandeville to Thomas, Robbie and their friends, while he removed his pocket watch, "but if we are to get the train home we must be going soon or we will miss the 4.30pm. train." There were sighs from all the youngsters. "Really children, we must start to make tracks for the station, if you would excuse the pun," he added, with a chuckle.

"What a day," commented Beth, when they settled in to their seats on the train once more, "and so full of surprises. Oh thank you, Mr Mandeville, for having taken us with you," and she gave him a kiss.

"My pleasure my dear, my pleasure," he replied. Beth noticed how tired he looked and tucked his blanket around him.

"Why don't you have a nap, we will wake you when we are getting close to Hayle?" she suggested.

He nodded and with the rhythmic rocking of the train he drifted off to sleep. Beth placed her finger to her lips and whispered to the boys to keep the noise down, while they looked out of the windows and talked about their day.

Five minutes before they were due to reach their station, Beth gently woke the old gentleman. The boys helped Mr Mandeville slowly off the train. Jake dashed off to collect the bath chair from where it had been stowed, while Beth checked, to ensure they had everything before she left the train carriage.

They helped Lewis's grandfather into his chair and wheeled him along the platform to the exit gate, being careful to hold it tightly, as they made their way down the slope to where the coach and horses awaited them.

All safely on board, they set off for the final part of their journey to Pennington and on to Wattle Peak. The children looked forward to the hot air balloon arriving at Wattle Peak about the middle of August - in three weeks' time.

---

# Chapter 14

## Time Away

Much to the Robertson children's delight, a last minute holiday in the Lake District with their parents had been arranged. Two weeks of fishing, canoeing and walking around the beautiful countryside, with its blue lakes, undulating hills and peaks. The boys looked forward to sleeping under canvas in a small tent. Beth thought them mad. She was happy to stay with her parents in a caravan, a short distance away and close to Lake Windermere.

The boys had rushed off, determined to set up the tent themselves. When their father went to have a look, Beth heard them state confidently, it was all done.

On the second night, Beth found it hard to sleep, as the rain pounded on the roof of the caravan, getting louder and louder as the rain got worse. Soon after she had finally dozed off, a tapping on the door of the main cabin, where she slept, woke her up. Creeping out of bed, she let in a bedraggled Mike and Jake. "We had forgotten to attach the ground sheet to the sides of the tent or to take into account the lie of the land," explained Mike, in a hushed tone, as Beth handed the boys towels, "and we were washed out." The two boys spent the rest of the night on the floor, with a few blankets and cushions, while the rain continued to patter on the roof.

The next morning, Beth gathered up the boys' bedding, sleeping bags and clothes and carried them out and pinned them on the washing line to dry. Meanwhile their father showed her brothers how to secure the ground sheet, so the water would not get in and helped them site the tent on a slight rise, so rain water would more likely flow around them. Luckily, the sun came out and soon dried off the bedding. The rest of the holiday remained hot and mainly dry.

Their father added fun to a picnic by showing them how to set up a camp fire. "Gather rocks or large stones to place around the fire," he instructed them, "that way the fire will not spread." They cooked the fish they had caught, skewered on sticks and hung over the flames, as potatoes wrapped in tinfoil baked in the glowing embers of the fire.

Jake was able to take a few more sailing lessons and had done quite well, proving he was a quick learner. There was a bonfire and barbeque on their last night at the campsite, along with dancing. Beth noticed the surprised look on their mother's face, when her children joined in the country dancing session. They had eagerly partnered their parents in the square dance. Mike had come out of his shell she saw, as he asked a pretty young girl to dance and showed her the steps. Beth smiled, now it would be her turn to tease Mike about his partner.

Their parents disappeared back to the caravan when the loud music of the disco started with its heavy beat, leaving their children and their vigorous gyrating on the dance floor.

Back home once more with their eighth visit fast approaching, Mike and Beth sat in the attic, discussing their hopes of having a flight in the hot air balloon.

"Shall we go Saturday or Sunday?" asked Mike, "we don't want to miss Robbie and Thomas; they had not been certain as to when they would actually arrive."

"Let's go on Saturday, rather early than too late. We could always visit again the next day if needs be," declared Beth and they agreed.

---

## Chapter 15

### Up Up and Away

When they arrived back in time at Wattle Peak on the Saturday, Beth and her brothers made their way up the path to the front door. Sadly, they couldn't see any sign of the balloon.

The maid who answered their knock was new and had been hired for a few days, while there would be guests. She told them they were expected in the large back garden.

Lewis rushed over to them, all smiles, when he caught sight of the dog and charged off down the garden with Sooty, while his grandfather looked on from where he sat in his bath-chair. Beth sat down by his side, as Jake and Mike settled for lying on the now short grass.

Beth looked around and commented how neat the garden looked. "Yes, a few sheep were borrowed and were grazing here, up to a few days ago," Wilkins informed her, as he cleared away the tea tray.

"What shall we do? It does not look like the balloon will arrive today," said Jake, stifling a yawn, as he lifted his head to look at his sister.

"They may still be here," replied Mr Mandeville, nodding his grey head and placing the local newspaper down on a little table. "The postcard I received did say they hoped to arrive on Saturday but maybe not until the evening. Oh, by the way, I've had the boat down by the jetty checked and varnished, since you were last here. Mike, you did say you could sail?"

"Why yes, we have had lessons," he replied.

"Please, please, would you take me out sailing?" said Lewis, as he flopped down beside the boys, exhausted from running about with Sooty.

"What do you say, Mr Mandeville. May we borrow the boat and take Lewis with us?" asked Mike.

"Well, so long as you wear the cork vests. I bought them from the Royal National Life Boat Institute while I was in Hayle. They are intended to keep you afloat if you were to fall into the sea. Wilkins will get them out for you."

Beth agreed to stay behind, as there were only three cork vests. Anyway, she wanted to have a word with cook about news of Simon, also she knew with her dress it would be difficult to get in and out of the boat, as well as taking up a lot of space. Beth promised them she would wave from the cliff top, if the balloon came in sight. She smiled to herself, secretly hoping to be alone, when Thomas arrived.

Lewis, Jake and Mike went off and made their way down the long cliff path to the creek, each carrying a life-vest.

"Well now, Beth, how about some tea and pancakes" said Mr Mandeville, grinning, "with cream and cook's strawberry jam." He licked his lips as his eyes lit up.

"Oh, that would be nice. Jake will be sorry to have missed such a treat. Shall I organise it with cook for you, as Wilkins has gone out front to check that the others made it safely to the boat?"

"Please," he replied. "Wilkins is very fond of Lewis you know and us of him. He has been with us many years."

Sooty wagged his tail and got up to follow Beth. "No, Sooty you stay here." The old gentleman put his hand out towards the little dog, so it ambled over to him, his tail wagging gently, knowing he would be fussed over. Beth smiled at the sight of them both, as she moved away.

Cook was soon busily preparing the pancakes, while she chatted with Beth. "Has Mrs Grant, the vicar's housekeeper, confirmed that the sweep is back in the area?" asked Beth.

"Apparently, he is due any day at the Judge's house. That sweep is a nasty bit of work, if you ask me," she confided.

"You're right," said Beth and told her what she had seen a while back at the Grand Fair.

When Beth returned to the garden carrying the tray, Wilkins was unfolding the tray stand. "Here, Miss Beth, let me take that while you sit yourself down. Oh, the boys got safely away," he confirmed, before he began to pour the tea. "They are heading along the coast towards Pennington and maybe as far as St Michael's Mount according to Mike, as there is a good breeze."

So Beth settled herself once more, next to Mr Mandeville, lifting her face to the warm sunshine "Did you see the announcement that there's to be a local by-election? Lord Humphreys has died, so we need a new Member of Parliament. It will be held in the autumn, on 25th October. It should be an interesting day, as people will come from miles around to listen to the candidates, but mostly to heckle," he chuckled.

Beth took the empty plates back to the kitchen. She saw cook's list of things to do and offered to go to Torrington for her, to collect two lobsters and a few crabs from Jacob, a fisherman, who lived on the quay. It was a nice day for a walk and she was more than happy to help cook, who was extremely busy preparing for the expected guests. It was a pleasant walk in the sunshine, along the cliff top path. She swung the wicker basket back and forth. The cool sea breeze felt good on her face, as she listened to the seagulls and watched the boats bobbing on the water.

Jacob, a man in his fifties, but still spritely, his hair was just beginning to show some grey, gave her a warm smile, when he heard who she was and the errand. "The parcel is ready," he said, "and I've included a pint of prawns for cook," and asked Beth to give cook his best regards, explaining he was very fond of her and winked. Beth smiled and wondered just how friendly they really were.

"There has been such a fuss over at the north end of the village, said Jacob. I've never seen anything like it, a hot air balloon, would you believe, a great big thing, if you please. It landed there because a wheel broke on the wagon that the balloonist's friends were travelling in."

"Oh, good," said Beth, "it must be Robbie, Thomas and friends on their way to Wattle Peak."

"Well, I never, you obviously know about it. I don't hold with these new-fangled things, you tell cook from me to keep well away from it." Beth laughed and thanked him for the shellfish and headed off to find the balloon.

It was in a field, still inflated and she blushed when she saw Thomas, who greeted her warmly, kissing her on each cheek in the French fashion.

"What are you doing here?" he asked surprised. She explained about her errand. "We should be off again shortly, as the wagon has been fixed and we just need to load it up again. Shall we take the shellfish back for you? It would save you carrying it," he offered.

"Why not take me with you, please?" said Beth, her eyes bright, "it's not far and I know the way."

"I thought you were joking about going for a flight. Most girls are frightened by heights," he said. "We won't want to have to come back down again because you don't like it."

"No fear of that," she said, standing on tiptoes to peer into the basket. She saw that it was partitioned with wicker panels, so it looked similar to a noughts and crosses board, the middle cross sections being slightly smaller than the corner squares and in the centre square the gas cylinder was secured. "I'm not scared of heights," she said confidently, "I have been up

Mount Snowdon with my parents, I shall be fine," In fact she had even been up the Eiffel Tower on a school trip but as she could not remember when it had been built, said nothing.

"You know, the landings are sometimes rough, it may be necessary to sit on the low seat with the straps across you, to help brace you for a crash landing. On occasions we have ended up on our backs or even hanging face down after a very bumpy landing. So are you still quite sure?" he said, with his head on one side.

"Of course I am, after all, you're still safe and sound after how many landings? so it can't be so bad. I shall take off my hooped petticoat from under my skirt and if you help me into the basket, all will be well," she replied, grinning at him. He smiled at her and she felt butterflies in her stomach - he was handsome.

"I like a girl with pluck. If you are in the basket by the time Robbie comes out of the smithies, it will be too late for him to argue. Pete and John have taken an empty gas cylinder to the post office, arranging to send it off to be refilled and then to be sent on to Hayle. They should be here any minute."

He turned his back and shielded her from view with his coat while she removed her hooped petticoat and he placed this garment, with the other goods, to go in the wagon. He helped her up the steps, climbing in ahead of her and waited while she'd gathered her skirt close about her, as it would drag on the floor without its support. He picked her up in his strong arms and carried her over the rim. Standing on the basket floor, she found the step on which she could perch to see over the side.

When Robbie arrived, he saw Beth and smiled, “Thomas always did have an eye for a pretty girl,” he said. Thomas grinned at him and explained that Beth would be their navigator. By the time Pete and John arrived the boys were ready to cast off.

“Won’t you wait for us to pack the wagon, so we can start off together?” queried Pete.

“Not necessary, we are turning inland,” explained Robbie, “and intend to approach Wattle Peak from behind the house and garden, while you are taking the shorter route along the cliff top road and should arrive before us. The balloon should be visible from the cliff top road most of the time.”

Pete let go of the ropes which were drawn up into the balloon by Robbie and Thomas. The balloon moved slowly and gracefully skyward, to the gasps of the gathered crowd. The sandbags had been adjusted to take into account that it held three passengers and the ropes moved into the empty corner section to help balance the weight. There was a whoosh of gas as they created more hot air, helping the balloon to rise steadily.

Beth waved to the people gathered around and watched as they, along with the wagon still being loaded, grew smaller and smaller. The balloon drifted in a northerly direction once it met the full force of the wind coming off the sea.

"It's so very quiet and calm," said Beth in awe, as they travelled along.

"Yes, we are travelling at the same speed as the wind, so you cannot hear it or feel it."

How pretty the town of Torrington looked, thought Beth, as she looked back towards it. In front she could also see the rise and fall of the cliffs with its pathway along the crescent bay. She looked out to sea but couldn't see the boys in the sailing dingy; perhaps they had already arrived back.

As they turned further inland they viewed little streams and several farms with their patchwork of fields, some golden others green and even red. In the distance there was a hill. densely covered by trees, so they rose higher to sail over it. Once cleared, they started to move down again, as a sudden gust took them close to the hill where they saw two figures in black, one much shorter than the other, emerge onto the open ground from the tree line. As the shadow of the balloon passed over these people, the man looked up and startled, missed his footing, and fell to the ground. The other one, a boy, ran off in fright, as the rope around his waist fell from the man's hand. The boy dropped his bundle of poles and brushes, as he sped off. Beth gasped, as she recognised the man as the sweep. He continued to cower at the sight of them. She watched, as Simon ran into a gully. He was having a coughing fit. She could see him holding his chest as he ran. The boy kept close to the gully wall before collapsing and crawling under a large bush.

Wattle Peak and beyond it Pennington were suddenly in sight. As Beth looked back, the man on his knees stood up shaking his fist at them, but she was sure he hadn't seen where Simon had gone. He yelled out Simon's name, cursing as he wandered back into the woods, searching.

Thomas and Robbie were busy adjusting the weight, to bring the balloon over towards Wattle Peak, the basket resisting the wind, just as planned. They opened the top vent on the canopy to let in the cold air, in order to descend.

"You really must watch out for the greenhouse in the grounds, it's near the end of the garden," Beth warned, shouting in earnest, as they went lower. "It's just beyond that row of trees!"

"Okay, okay but where are Pete and John?" queried Robbie anxiously, "they should have been in the garden by now."

"Oh, no. I can see them. They are still on the cliff top road stuck behind a huge flock of geese, with their keeper," replied Beth, her face screwed up in horror.

"Oh lor, we may have to use the anchor to stop the balloon, which will tear up the garden somewhat."

"It can't be helped," replied Thomas. There was a sudden gust just as they neared the garden which took them uncontrollably towards the greenhouse. "Up, Robbie, up," he yelled and Robbie opened the gas up full, "now release the sand bags your side," and Thomas did the same, hoping no-one was below them. It worked and the balloon began to rise sharply. They missed the greenhouse by inches, but now they were too high to land in the garden. Those precious seconds meant, in turn, they couldn't use the anchor, so would have to go over the roof of the house that loomed ahead of them, as Mr Mandeville and Wilkins looked up in alarm.

"Keep the gas going at full blast Robbie, we will have to go over the house, it's the only way! Beth, you may need to strap in," he called urgently.

They just cleared the roof, hearing the basket scrapping against the ridge tiles, as they crawled over it. Beth had her eyes closed; when opening them again she saw the sailing dingy out in the bay. Suddenly, the thermal breezes used by the seagulls to soar over the cliffs, lifted the balloon high into the air. Beth pulled down the seat ready to strap herself in.

It was obvious to Beth, when she glanced at Robbie and Thomas face's, that they had been unaware the that Georgian house was so close to the cliff edge.

Robbie let cold air into the canopy once more, "You must get strapped in, Beth," commanded Thomas. She did so this time, but then could not see anything, other than the side of the basket. Her heart beat faster, as she gripped the straps, fearing they had to go out over the cliffs and probably over the sea. The words 'next stop America' came into her mind, 'Oh, Lord, help us,' she thought. "Can you take the balloon down quickly, you may be able to land in the creek, if you move to the left," she said, picturing what was she knew lay below and felt the balloon descending, air turbulence rocking them, as the thermals and cross winds caught it.

"Oh no, not quick enough," shouted Thomas, "stop the cold air, we have missed the creek and I'm sorry to say, Beth, we are out over the sea. There's a dinghy sailing below, we've just passed over it; the occupants must have seen us, as they have turned and are sailing in our direction."

"The dinghy," shouted Beth, "that must be Mike, Jake and Lewis. Maybe they can help."

"Yes, you're right, I'll drop a sandbag tied to the anchor and trail it in the water behind us it could slow us down, so they can catch up with us. Where is the loud hailer?" cried Robbie frustrated, searching frantically in the small section to his right. "Oh, here it is." He picked it up and leaned over the side, lifting it to his lips, "Mike, can you grab the rope?" he yelled, pointing towards the rope trailing in the water, "and pull us towards the cliffs once more?" Mike gave the thumbs up, as he got Jake to lean over and reach for it, while he guided the boat.

"Oh, no," cried Jake, "I can't reach."

"I'll turn us around," replied Mike, trying to keep calm and swiftly brought the boat about. On the second pass, Jake caught it.

"Got it," he shouted.

"Well done, Jake, now tie the rope to the ring at the front of the boat." Having done so the boat almost ground to a halt, but thankfully the balloon had stopped drifting out to sea. Mike and Jake got out the oars and started to row back to land.

Looking to the shore, they saw Pete and John on the sand, waiting to help. The balloon was still 20 feet up in the air.

Pete and John joined them at the jetty, as the dingy pulled in. The balloon was lowered until they could pull it over to the jetty and tie it there, securely.

A much relieved Robbie and Thomas climbed out and then Beth stood up a little shakily, to the horror of Mike, Lewis, and Jake, who had no idea she was in there and had been in such danger. Robbie jumped back in and lifted Beth over the side into Thomas's arms.

She smiled at him, "All's well then," she said.

"You are one brave lass," he replied and they laughed together. "I will carry you up the cliff path." He left the boys to figure out how to bring the balloon safely up to the cliff top.

At the top of the cliff, Mr Mandeville, cook and Wilkins waited, as Thomas carried her to the house. Cook followed, having retrieved the hooped petticoat from the wagon, as Beth requested.

Mr Mandeville asked Thomas what went wrong. "It was mainly the wind and those thermals; we have not had to deal with such forces before and would not have put Beth in such danger had we known about them," he apologised.

Pete and John figured out a way, using ropes, which would allow the still inflated balloon to be brought up past the cliff face. Eventually they guided it up on to the top path. There they would deflate it and pack it away, having decided it was too dangerous to use there again and would, in future, keep at least a quarter of a mile from the coast if there were cliffs involved.

"We hope to restart our journey from the north side of Pennington tomorrow or maybe the following day" declared Thomas. Mike's face fell and Beth knew he was thinking he might not get his trip after all.

"We hope to find the time to come back during the next few days to see you off," said Beth, Mike looked at her puzzled then smiled as he realised it meant he would get his flight.

After dinner, the trio said their goodbyes and set off for home once more, with Sooty by their side. Beth explained, as they entered the attic that she had seen Simon and he would need their help. Luckily the weather was good at the moment, so he should survive, as it was still warm at night. So it was agreed that they would come back early on the morrow, before the Mandeville household was up, to try to find Simon, praying Mr Grimshaw had not already found him.

---

## Chapter 16

### Rescue

When they arrived home they told their parents they just had been given spare tickets for a day trip to a safari park and that the outing would be the following day. It was a youth club outing and it would mean a very early start and they might be back late. Their parents were happy for them to go, but reminded them to stick together when coming home.

At 5.30am the children still yawning quietly entered the kitchen for breakfast. Mum had left their cereal bowls ready-filled, plus sandwiches in the fridge. As the forecast predicted rain and windy conditions, there was soup to be heated and put into the flasks on the table.

"Good old mum," said Jake, as he poured milk on his cereal. Soon they were ready and picked up what they needed and headed off to the attic in the old farmhouse. Mike closed the front door of the main house, softly, using the key, so as to make no noise. A change of clothes and they were ready, once more, to venture into Victorian times.

"The dawn has just broken," said Beth quietly as the trio emerged from the attic.

"There's a light on in the kitchen so cook must be up and already baking bread," whispered Jake, returning from checking that the wagon still stood on the drive near the front door, as he rubbed the remaining sleep out of the corners of his eyes. Turning in the opposite direction, they very quietly moved towards the side gate. Startled on hearing loud noises coming from the stable block, they stopped dead. Beth's hand went to her throat, as she held her breath letting it out with a low sigh, when a horse popped its head over the stable door. They had forgotten the wagon horses would be there.

Soon they were out of the gate and hurrying along the path. Beth had explained they needed to make their way along the cliff top roadway, towards Torrington before turning inland, once they saw the wooded area on the hill. Ten minutes later, they crossed a ditch, using a wide tree trunk that had been placed there for the purpose and headed up the hill towards the wood.

"It's somewhere along here," called Beth, trying to picture the wood as she had seen it from above. She moved over the crest of the hill and finally saw the gully. "Here it is," she cried, carefully making her way down the slope. As she made her way along she held on to the bushes, searching under each of the larger ones, until she saw a foot and waved the boys to come and join her.

The lad was rather dirty, due to the soot ground into his skin and clothes. He appeared to be fast asleep, or so they thought, until they gently tried to wake him and found he was unconscious.

Mike had brought along a blanket. It was hung over one of his shoulders, the ends held close to his body with the aid of the string tied around his waist. He had said he thought it might be needed. He'd untied the string and wound it around his fingers, then placed it in his pocket, before shrugging the blanket off his shoulder. They lifted the boy into a sitting position and placed the blanket around Simon's shoulders, before leaning him back against Mike.

"He's very hot," said Beth, concerned. Jake, who had brought a thick glass lemonade bottle full of water, suggested they try to give him drink. Beth held the bottle to Simon's lips and he swallowed just a little, his eyes fluttered open briefly and he smiled at her before closing his eyes again.

"He won't be able to walk," said Beth worried.

"I know," replied Mike, "we might have to take him back to the attic. I've left some aspirin hidden in a tin box. Beth had wondered what the box contained. "We still have those straw pallets, the ones used by the decorators, so we could lay him on those."

"How do we get him back though," said Jake, scratching his head.

"Carry him in the blanket," suggested Mike and the others agreed.

"Until we get him out of the gully, Beth and I will take the back section," said Mike, taking control. "Jake, you will have to hold the two front corners, while we climb up the slope."

They laid the blanket out and folded it in half before gingerly lifting the boy between them, trying not to get too dirty. Simon was thin, so he was much lighter than they expected. They grabbed hold of the blanket corners and lifted him up, Beth and Mike taking most of the weight as they carefully climbed out of the gully.

"We must keep below the crest of the hill," warned Beth, "until we get to near Wattle Peak."

They stopped every now and then, to rest their arms and to change places. They ventured over the rise, when they thought they were close to the house, making for the end of the garden, crossing via stepping stones over the stream, the same one that later created the waterfall, that cascaded over the cliff into the creek below. They kept close to the hedge and then the wall around the grounds of Wattle Peak, so as not to be seen from the back windows. They hoped no one would come along the road from Torrington, as they could easily be seen from that direction. Jake volunteered to see if the coast was clear before they headed on to the roadway and entered the small gate. He swiftly returned to confirm all was quiet. They moved tiredly past the front wall as far as the little gate. Beth went through first, leaving Jake to carry the front end of their burden through, while Mike followed up with the other end as quickly as possible. However, as Jake struggled through the opening, they heard the clip clop of a cart-horse getting closer. It was coming from the Pennington's direction, "It must be the milk cart, keep going," urged Beth, as they hurried through the gateway and into the tack room. Once there they kept out of sight and kept very quiet.

The milkman came through the gate, looked around, shrugged, and walked up to the kitchen door, leaving four quart cans, before picking up two empty ones. Once the footsteps receded, they carefully made their way to the stairs. It was a slow job. Thankfully, they reached the top without mishap and placed Simon on a pallet.

"He needs a wash," said Beth, "and new clothes. There are almost more holes than material in his trousers. Jake, keep away from the windows," said Beth, crossly. Jake ducked down. "We don't want anyone coming up to see who's here."

"What do we do with him now?" Jake asked.

"We'll clean him up for a start. Do you think you could borrow two buckets from the stable and fill them with water from the stream and… not get caught?"

"Of course, leave it to me," Jake replied, as he quietly went down the stairs.

Beth disappeared into the other room and returned with a maid's old apron that had been left in the cupboard and the two sheets, used by Jake and Mike when playing at ghosts to get rid of the decorators. Beth had removed any remaining plaster dust before she had placed them in the washing machine, while her mum was out, so she knew they were clean. She decided that this time she would not chide Mike for not having put them back in the stables, as he should have done. He had a habit of promising to do things and then forgetting. One sheet would be used as part of the bedding for Simon, once he was clean, the other she began tearing up to use as flannels, towels and some for cold compresses. She remembered Alicia telling her this was done to her and Lucinda when they had cholera, back in Georgian times.

She fastened the thick calico apron around her to protect her dress and sorted through the rags, ready for her task. She shook the blanket out and brushed off some of the soot before turning the still slightly dirty side in and folding it in half, for use in due course.

Mike brought up an old enamelled washing bowl he found tucked away in the corner of the tack room.

"It's a pity the shops are closed as its Sunday," said Beth, speaking her thoughts out loud, "but maybe the vicar can help. Mike, can you go and visit him, to see if he has some old clothes that might fit Simon? Offer to buy them but don't tell him who they are actually for, so that he won't have to tell any lies, if questioned. Oh! and ask for some soap."

"You think the Sweep will still be searching then?"

"Oh, yes," she replied.

Jake brought the buckets up the stairs, one at a time.

"If you go now Mike, you will catch the vicar before he starts his Sunday services. Should you meet any of the Mandeville's guests in town, tell them you are on an errand and that Jake and I should be along later."

***

Mike cautiously moved downstairs and out along the cliff top road, hurrying up the lane leading to the vicar's house and the church. On his way, he saw the grubby sweep asking people if they had seen his apprentice.

Mike poked his head around the church door, searching for the Reverend Barclay and found him busily putting out the hymn books, ready for use.

"Well you're keen, there's still quite a while before the service," said the vicar, looking surprised "I don't get many youngsters for the eight o'clock one."

"Sorry to disappoint you, vicar, but I have only come for your help. I urgently need some clothes for a boy about nine years old, I will pay for them."

"Who are they for?"

"Best I don't say for now," said Mike, "but it is in a good cause and I would be grateful if you would keep the matter quiet."

"Well, as I will be busy for some time, it would be best if you go and see my housekeeper, she will help you sort out what you need. We had some clothes given us a few days ago, to be passed on to the poor or sold to bring in funds."

"Thank you," said Mike, waving goodbye.

Mike hurried off to the vicarage and there Mrs Grant helped him find what he needed along with some soap. She laid out a sheet of brown paper to make a parcel for him and Mike helped to fold the clothes before placing some money on the table.

"That's far too much," she said.

"Call it a donation and please keep it between you, me and the vicar, that I bought these, yes?"

"Yes, if you say so," she replied puzzled.

"Oh, you wouldn't have anything for a bad chest, would you, it's for Jake," said Mike. "The shops won't be open until tomorrow and none of us are able to get any sleep at home with all the coughing," he said, giving a yawn.

"Well, there's a jar of chest ointment you can have, it's been opened for a while and would be thrown away soon, so you're welcome to it," said Mrs Grant, moving towards a cupboard and lifting out a green jar. "You could give him some of this as well, it will help him sleep at night; it has laudanum in it, so do not exceed the dosage," and she added the jar and a smaller blue bottle to the parcel before tying it securely. He thanked her and hurried away.

***

Meanwhile Beth had been applying cold compresses to Simon's head and had fed him a little soup, with an aspirin in it. After washing his face and hands, they took off his jacket. With Jake's help, she washed Simon's upper body with cold water, all helping to bring down his temperature. Soon the water and flannels were black. His breathing still sounded laboured.

Whistling, Mike walked back to Wattle Peak, with the parcel under his arm. It was just before nine o'clock when he turned into the gate and he walked straight into Pete and John, busily mucking out the stables.

"My, you're up and about early," said Pete, "so where are the other two?"

"Oh, they will be along later," Mike replied, "I've been on an errand," indicating the parcel.

Beth and Jake heard what was being said below but were alarmed when the door to the tack room was opened. They relaxed on hearing Mike's voice, "Let me give you a hand with the work," said Mike, as he opened the tack room door further still, "I'll just leave my jacket and the parcel in the tack room for now and deliver it later." He stepped inside and popped the parcel on the stairs, with his jacket on top, "I had intended to I would drop in and see you on my way back, so as to find out what the plans are for the balloon." The voices then died away, as the door closed. Both Jake and Beth sighed with relief. Jake crept down the stairs and brought the parcel up to Beth. Inside, she found the soap and set about gently re-washing Simon's face, now able to give him a proper wash. Jake removed his jacket and rolled up his shirt sleeves, needing to keep them clean. He helped hold Simon's head, supporting it for Beth, over the edge of the pallet and basin, while she washed his hair. Gradually, the fairness of his hair became visible and she dried it as best she could with a piece of the sheet. She hung the pieces of sheeting she had used, over the banister at the top of the stairs, to dry. The dirty water had been poured back into one bucket, to be got rid of later. Jake removed Simon's trousers for her under a large piece of cloth and he washed the rest of his body before they moved him onto the other clean pallet, where Jake placed a nightshirt over Simon's head and thin body. As it was a rather warm day, they left him as he was for now, as they daren't open the window. Beth read the label on the green jar and decided to use the chest ointment on Simon. As the strong smell assailed her nose reminding her of the gel mother had rubbed onto her own chest, when she had a cough after flu several years ago. Beth wiped her hands on a rag and left it close to Simon, so the vapour from it would help his breathing. It smelt like eucalyptus, she thought.

Simon suddenly woke up, coughing and Beth gave him some rag to use as a hankie, as he managed to bring up some of the muck from his chest, the effort leaving him so exhausted, that he immediately dozed off again but his breathing had become less laboured.

They opened a flask and settled to drink some soup, remembering that the weather, back home, had not been very warm over the last few days, the soup would have been very welcome on their so called safari park trip. They unpacked a sandwich each and tucked in, while waiting for Mike. Simon was fast asleep, his face still slightly flushed but his temperature was coming down.

Beth decided to give him some of the sleeping draught next time he woke but mindful of the warning on the bottle about giving the correct dose, she carefully measured one capful into a little water. When Simon opened his eyes, he was still in a daze. She gave him some soup from one of the tin mugs, left by the decorators, before giving him the prepared sleeping draught. She remembered her mother saying 'sleep helps to mend an ailing body.'

It was shortly before noon, when Mike finally came quietly up the stairs, to check out what had been happening with Simon, while he'd been away.

"You took your time," said Beth, a little irritated.

"Well, I gave them a hand, carrying some bales and some sacks of oats into the stables. Then I helped them sort out the wagon, repacking everything, by which time tea and biscuits were on offer and I needed a drink."

"So, when will they be moving the balloon?" asked Jake.

"Good news. They don't intend to move it until tomorrow. They will launch it from the field near the church, around 1pm, then hope to head northeast towards Hayle. They have promised me a flight, if I can get someone to bring me back. Perhaps the vicar would help?" Mike's face brightened. "I'll stay with Simon, if you and Jake would like to visit the Mandeville's for a while; lunch will be ready soon. Just tell them that you met me on my way home with my parcel and that they may see me this evening."

"Yes, a good idea," replied Jake, with a grin, "I'm dying for a pee."

"There's a gazunder down in the tack room; it must have been left here for the decorators and it looks clean," said Mike.

"A what?" queried Jake.

"He means a china chamber pot, you know, a po," explained Beth, grinning.

"Oh yes, I saw one of those in an antique shop; it had an eye painted in the bottom of it," he replied and he started to giggle, which started them all off.

"It could be useful for Simon," responded Beth, her face serious once more. "Now we have rescued him, what do we do with him?"

"We'll think of something," replied Jake, looking glum. "Oh, by the way, I've wrapped his old clothes in the brown paper and tied it up; we will need to get rid of those and the dirty water in the buckets. Beth, when we leave, if you keep watch, I'll pour the water onto the flower bed by the side of the farmhouse."

"Good idea. There is actually a tap at the back of the stable yard, I saw it earlier," said Mike, "so wash them out, refill one and leave it inside the tack room."

Beth used the now dry cloth, to make sure she had got rid of any remaining soot on the floor, gingerly using her foot to move the cloth around, having lifted the hem of her skirt, so it would not get it dirty. When she turned, Mike was carefully rolling up the dirty pallet. Jake put two flasks on the shelves in the cupboard along with some of the sandwiches and hid them with the cloths, but left one flask out with some sandwiches for Mike, as he would miss lunch.

As agreed, Mike kept a lookout and all went well. Soon Beth and Jake were at the front door and being whisked inside. Lewis ran to greet them. They were pleased to be asked to stay for lunch. The youngsters all sat together listening to the plans the four young men made for their next trip and were even allowed to examine their maps. John would be going up on the next trip, instead of Robbie, a reward he received every now and then for being part of the support staff on the trip. Pete had only been up once and found he was not keen on heights, so was happier on the ground.

The evening was approaching when Beth excused herself, stating she wanted a word with cook and disappeared, leaving them playing a game. As she entered the large kitchen, cook stood at the enormous wooden table with several of her prepared dishes arranged at one end. The pots and pans shone brightly hanging on hooks around the room. The door to the walk-in pantry stood ajar, where could be seen blue jars of varying heights on a high shelf and a large stone shelf that helped to keep things cool. Other shelves were stacked with many paper packets, jam jars, preserves and empty bowls sat, one inside another.

"Hello Beth, everything alright? You must be the centre of attention in there, as the only young lady," she teased.

"Hardly, they're all too busy with their maps or playing a game," she said, with a sigh.

"Will Mike be back in time for high tea, about six o'clock? As it's a hot day, it was decided it would be more appropriate than a heavy meal, such as a roast.

"I doubt it," replied Beth. "Cook," said Beth, hesitantly, "do you know of anyone who might need a nine year old boy, to help out with chores for his keep, someone who would not ill-treat him?"

Cook looked at her thoughtfully for a moment. "The caretaker here is not only hard of hearing but his eyesight is getting worse. He needs someone to let him know when to open the gates, plus we need help with the garden. The boy could live with him in the farmhouse. Perhaps Mr Mandeville would be willing to take him on but with his son returning in the New Year, he might want to leave such matters to him? How soon would he need the job?"

"He isn't very well at present, so perhaps in a week or two." replied Beth, "once he's got his strength back."

"With the winter coming, I could do with help making up the fires, bringing in the coal and such. Let me have a quiet word with Wilkins first, when I think the moment's right. We often have a cup of tea together, last thing at night."

"Oh, thanks cook," said Beth, and planted a kiss on her cheek.

"Get away with you; I've made no promises, remember."

Sometime after the evening meal, Jake and Beth decided it was time they made tracks for home and after saying their goodbyes, promised to be back the next day. Once out of the front door, they quickly returned to the attic.

"How's he been?" asked Beth, as soon as she reached Simon's side.

"He's quiet now; he was coughing earlier, so I gave him another aspirin for the pain. He's had a drop more soup and ate a little of my sandwich."

Beth prepared another draught of the sleeping potion, for when it would be needed, while she told them what cook had said about finding Simon work. Though pleased with this possibility, they sat, worriedly, trying to decide what to do about Simon that night. Would it be alright to leave him on his own?

***

"I'll see you in a short while," said Mike, picking up a lamp, as it would be dark soon. "I wanted to see Thomas, Robbie and the other lads about tomorrow's balloon flight."

Just as Mike was about to open the tack room door, Jake called down the stairs, “The sweep, Mr Grimshaw, is coming towards the farmhouse!”

Mike quickly left the tack room, closing the door as he did so and made for the path, leading to the main house. Suddenly, he heard the sweep shouting, he had entered via the small gate and now stood on the path.

“I know he’s in there,” yelled the sweep at Mike, who turned to face him. The sweep pointed to the farmhouse with his stick. “You have stolen my property,” and he shook the stick at Mike, as he advanced towards him.

“Steady on,” said Mike, backing away from him fearfully, “what are you on about, what property?” To Mike’s relief he heard the front door of the Georgian house open and Wilkins, together with the four lads, made their way towards him and surrounded the sweep.

“What’s this all about my, good man?” asked Wilkins, drawing himself up to his full height.

“You know full well and don’t you ‘good man’ me,” he barked, as he made his way towards the tack room door. “You have my lad, Simon, and I want him back, I saw him at the upstairs window of the farmhouse a minute ago.” Drats, you are a fool Jake, thought Mike.

“Why would I have your lad and he is a person not your ‘personal property,’” said Mike, annoyed.

“You thought you got away with it, didn’t you? But I know that your sister had the vicar make enquires about Simon and his family and before that you were overheard at the fair talking about him. I have friends who keep me informed. Now, out of my way!" He made for the door and started to push it open.

"Oh, no you don't!" said Wilkins, pulling him away from the open door, "that's not enough evidence to accuse Mike of anything. When did you lose sight of Simon?"

"Yesterday afternoon, when these people here," he pointed to Robbie and Thomas, "scared me half to death and nearly knocked me down with their infernal flying contraption. They made me lose a hold of my rope, attached to the boy. I paid good money for him," he said, angrily shaking his stick again.

"Well then, he has had plenty of time to start making his way to his family," said Wilkins.

"Oh no, he hasn't the strength for that and anyway I have been to see them, in case he got a lift, he's… not… there..," he said leering at Mike. "You can't wriggle out of it, you were seen with my lad, out early this morning."

"Seen doing what and by whom?" said Mike, now a little scared, but putting on a brave face.

"You were seen by the milkman, about 6.30am, carrying a heavy object, wrapped in something and you carried it through this gate, so what have you to say to that?"

The others all looked at Mike, puzzled, Pete and John, he knew, had seen him around early and that he had already completed an errand by the time they saw him at about 8.30 am.

"Oh dear, I will have to come clean," Mike said, turning to Wilkins, "I know we should have asked first but it was so early, so we took a chance and brought Sooty into the tack room, as he was injured. We borrowed an old dust sheet and carried him back here, as it's a lot closer than home."

"A likely story," said Grimshaw waving his head from side to side.

Mike ignored him, "You see we lost Sooty yesterday evening near the woods and we had to give up looking when it became too dark. We hoped he might have gone home but he wasn't there and our aunt wouldn't let us go back in the dark to find him even with a lamp. We came out very early this morning, as we thought he must be hurt as he still hadn't come home. When we found him, we weren't sure what his injuries were, so we carried him here, carefully in an old sheet, to examine him and it turned out it was only a knock to the head, and no bones were broken. However, he was spark out and it was a while before he came round. We didn't want to upset Lewis or Mr Mandeville, by saying anything neither could we risk Lewis, maybe accidently touching a sore spot, as that might have caused the dog to snap. Once we knew we wouldn't cause him any pain by moving him again, Jake and Beth took him back home. He's a little wobbly and still has a lump on his head."

"Don't give me that rubbish!" howled Grimshaw, "I am not falling for your fanciful story, I saw a face at the window and I'm not leaving until I get him back."

“We will settle it one way or another, let’s go up to the attic,” said Robbie annoyed by the whole business and leading the way with Mr Grimshaw following.

“The room is empty, I don’t believe it,” Grimshaw blustered. “Wait a minute this room is not square but the building is. He’s hidden in here somewhere. I’ve been in many houses over the years that had priest holes.” He walked over to the panelling and made his way along, tapping and pushing as he went. When he reached the panels at the end, he pushed the door open. Mike, standing at the top of the stairs, looked on in horror. A strange shudder went through him.

“Didn’t I tell you,” exclaimed Grimshaw in triumph, but on entering the narrow room he found it empty and, despite opening every cupboard, failed to find anyone hiding inside. He looked dumbfounded. “I know I saw something,” he growled.

Wilkins laughed, “You must have seen our resident ghosts, the ones the decorators saw. Didn’t you hear about it at the inn? Oh, but you weren’t in the area then, were you, why not ask them about it? Come to think of it, the ghosts have only ever been seen by scoundrels! Now, out of here and don’t come back,” he cried, pushing Grimshaw towards the stairs.

“Maybe he’s in the main house?”

“Enough of this - just go!” Wilkins commanded. “You have my word he’s not there.”

“I could get the police officer to search the place.” muttered Grimshaw, as he descended the stairs and went outside, followed by the others.

“I assume, Mr Grimshaw,” said Mike, “that you are unaware that my uncle is the Lord Chief Justice, William Erle? He would be interested to hear how you have been flouting the law and how the local justice has broken the same laws too. That’s why my sister was making enquiries, so as to establish the facts. You know full well, children are no longer allowed to climb chimneys and that you’re not allowed to employ any lad under 10 years old to work for you, or as your apprentice. Be warned, I’ll tell him about all this, when I return to London at the end of the year. I may even ask my father to write to him before then, if I ever see you again.” Grimshaw frightened, looked at Mike, his face twisted with hatred.

“It sounds as if it would be wise for you to move on to somewhere far from here,” said Wilkins, pushing him closer to the gate. “You’re lucky I don’t have the master lay a charge against you for disturbing the peace.”

Grimshaw growled once more and slunk out of the small gate, hurrying away towards Pennington. They watched him until he’s was out of sight.

“Come on Mike, let’s have some tea before you make for home. It’s best to give Grimshaw plenty of time to be away from here before you leave,” said Robbie, “And you can tell us how you know so much about the law.”

"Sorry, we did not tell you about the dog," said Mike to Wilkins, as they walked quickly to the main house.

"That's alright, Mike."

Wilkins then made for the kitchen. He said he would let cook know what all the excitement was about and arrange for tea and biscuits.

While munching a biscuit, Mike explained that the vicar had looked up the law for him and that William Erle was not, in fact, his uncle. They all laughed, when recalling the look on Grimshaw's face, when Mike threatened him with the law.

As Mike finished his tea, he worried as to where he would spend the night, as he was unable to get home - the trunk had gone!

---

## Chapter 17

### Unexpected Journey

Beth, on hearing the commotion downstairs and fearing trouble, said "Quick," to Jake, "help me to drag Simon on the straw pallet, into the narrow room. They held their breath, once inside, as they heard many footsteps on the stairs and in the attic. Jake's eyes widened when they heard Grimshaw shouting about a hidden room. He grabbed Beth's arm, when he heard the tapping on the walls. "Hurry," whispered Beth, into Jake's ear, "help me lift Simon up." They lifted Simon, so as to hold him between them, along with the pallet and blanket. Placing the sleeping draught bottle safely in Jake's pocket, she swiftly opened the trunk. Beth prayed, as she took a chance, hoping that only those in the same room and close to the trunk, would travel back in time. As the sparkles stop, Beth strained her ears, but no sound could be heard. Opening the door she gave a big she sigh when she found that there was no one in the room.

"Phew, I thought we would be caught," said Jake, as they laid Simon down once more and made him comfortable.

It was 7.30pm at home they realised, on looking at their watches. "If we leave Simon in the narrow room, will he be alright?" queried a frowning Jake.

"Yes, if we wait until 10.30pm and then give him his sleeping draught," said Beth. "It should be okay, as mum and dad are expecting us to be late and I think I know how we can get indoors, without them knowing there are just the two of us," She then checked that their torches were working, so when it became dark, they wouldn't have to put on the lights.

At 10.30pm, while Beth gave the sleeping draught to Simon. Jake changed back into his own clothes, in the main room. "Jake, would you sneak into the garage and fill up our jug with water from the old sink?" He nodded and went to find the key for the door that led into the old parlour, now his dad's work shop-com-garage and from there into the garage, with its sink and loo. Jake carefully moved around the car, so as not to set the alarm off and made his way back upstairs with the water. Meantime, Beth had changed her clothes, in the main room.

"I think we had better leave him in the narrow room. If he woke up in this room, he would never understand the things we have in here."

"Good idea. How long do we dare leave him there on his own?" asked Jake.

"The draught lasts about 6 hours so, 4.30am," said Beth, pacing up and down, "but as it will be dark then, should he stir, he's not likely to get up. I think we could safely leave it until 5am and then give him some more sleeping draught." She stopped and smiled, “My nightdress and dressing gown, being long, won’t look so strange to him if I pop back then.”

“I wonder if Mike will remember the sandwiches in the cupboard, although the soup will be cold by now,” said Jake. I daresay he would have sheltered for the night in the attic, that’s what I would have done.” Trust Jake to remember the food first, thought Beth and nodded, she was confident Jake was right.

The roadway had been wet, when they had arrived back, but by the time they left the attic it had all dried up. Once they opened the front door, Jake quickly and noisily opened the door to the office, as Beth said, loudly, “Home at last.” Their mother then popped her head out of her bedroom door. Beth knew she would not sleep until she knew they had safely arrived home.

“Had a good time,” she called, “where’s Mike?”

“Yes, it was a really good day, Mum. Mike’s getting Sooty, to let him have a piddle in the garden,” said Jake, heading for the kitchen, as Beth push the front door closed.

Beth, looking up at her mother, and said, “I’m just going to make us a cup of hot milk, would you like some?”

“No, thank you, dear. Night, night and don’t forget to turn out the lights and make sure the front door is locked,” and with this she yawned and made her way back to bed.

“Night, Mum,” replied Beth, making for the kitchen.

Jake went back to the front door with Sooty and watched, as the light went out in his parent's room, before actually taking Sooty outside, returning a few minutes later closing the front door, loudly enough to be heard.

"We're in the kitchen, Mike," called Beth.

"Okay," replied Jake softly, as he entered the kitchen, trying hard to sound like Mike.

Beth and Jake drank their milk and waited a while before going to bed. Beth set her alarm to go off at 4.45 am, placing it under her pillow. Yet another early morning she thought and yawned sleepily.

Beth woke with a start, immediately switching off the alarm. She struggled out of bed and into her slippers and dressing gown. Yawning, she hurried down stairs and into the kitchen. There, Beth picked up a plate on which there were a few slices of bread and jam that she'd prepared before going to bed. These she had covered with another plate, to keep them fresh and took them with her to the attic. Beth remembered to take a few clean rags for Simon to use as hankies. Sooty was by her side, as she crept out of the house.

Beth quietly entered the attic's narrow room, where she saw Simon covered by an old blanket, he raised himself up sleepily on one elbow and looked up at her, "Take it easy," she said, "here's some bread and jam; you must be hungry."

Just then, Sooty poked his head around her dressing-gown and moved towards Simon, wagging his tail. Simon smiled, but soon began coughing again, holding his stomach, which ached from all the coughing. Once this eased, Sooty started to wash Simon's face and the lad laughed. "It tickles," he said, as he stroked the dog's head.

"Where am I? Who washed me and where are my clothes?" he blushed.

"You're safe for now, at Wattle Peak," said Beth. "I'm Beth. My brothers and I found you and we brought you here. You will meet my brother, Jake, in a while and Mike maybe later. Mr Grimshaw was still searching for you last night, so you must stay in this room for now and keep away from the windows, even if you hear some noises outside or in the next room, please, just stay in here. My brother Jake, helped to wash you and we have some new clothes for you."

"Some new clothes," queried Simon, with a smile.

"Yes. Here's some water, so tuck into the bread and jam," she urged.

He ate it eagerly and then Beth put some Vic rub on his chest, which she had brought over from their bathroom cupboard. She had found a chamber pot in her mother's kitchen and removed the potted plant from inside it. Beth placed it near to Simon with a cloth over it, indicating that it was there, if he needed it. Finally, she gave him the sleeping draught.

"I will leave you now," she said, "and I'll see you later. Try to go back to sleep; you must rest."

"Thank you," he replied drowsily.

Beth headed back to her home. She was startled, when her mother, leaving the bathroom, spotted her in the hall.

"Oh Beth, it's you, I thought I heard someone about," she called, puzzled.

"Oh, I heard Sooty whine when I came down for some water, so I took him out for his morning wee. I'll just clean his feet, before I go back to bed."

They then both yawned and her mother went back to her own room.

***

Mike, as Jake and Beth anticipated back in Victorian times, had crept up to the dark attic, grateful for the moonlight and to spend the night there alone. He found the clean dust sheet they had intended to use on Simon and having first removed his trousers and jacket, so as not to look a mess the next morning, he wrapped the sheet around himself, the summer's night still quite warm. This protected him from the dirty smudges on the straw pallet, which he unrolled once more, this time for his own use and eventually he dozed off.

He woke early, about 6am, to the sound of cook calling quietly up the stairs, "Breakfast, Mike." He then heard the door close and crept downstairs, to see a tray laden with two teas and a plate full of buttered crumpets, with a pot of jam beside them.

He gratefully took the tray upstairs and tucked in, wondering if anyone else had guessed he spent the night there.

At about 9am Mike noticed the door to the narrow room open and saw Beth cautiously poke her head out, before she moved into the main room, “Morning Mike.” she said, as Jake followed her out into the main room, “sorry about having to leave you last night.”

“Am I glad you’re back,” the relief showed on his face. “How’s Simon?”

“A lot better; the rest has done him a lot of good. He’s still asleep, which made it easier for us to handle him, as we brought him back with us.”

“I brought you half a bacon sandwich, but I see you don’t need it,” said Jake, who had noticed the empty cups and a plate, with a few crumpets still left on it. “Where did all those come from?”

Mike filled them in on what occurred, after they had left and how, hopefully, Grimshaw the sweep, had left for good.

“Cook must have guessed I was here and by the amount of crumpets and two cups she left me, she must have assumed I had Simon with me. What happened at home, hasn’t Mum missed me?”

Jake explained what had happened, back home the night before. "Then this morning we convinced Mum you had gone out very early, to meet some new friends you'd made on our journey to the safari Park and that you were joining them at the swimming pool, at the new leisure centre, for an early morning swim. We told her, that later you intended to join them for a free day's try-out at its gym and other facilities, to see if you wanted to become a member. So, if she asks, that's the story."

"Simon should be awake soon," said Beth, "he knows he needs to stay in the narrow room, for the moment, in case Grimshaw is around. I need to speak to cook and see what we can do for Simon. I know you want to go on that flight later today, Mike, so Jake, do you think you could stay and keep Simon company?"

Jake nodded, "Yes, if you want and I will give him the bacon sandwich, also the crumpets, when he wakes up and help him dress."

"We need to bring the trunk out of the narrow room otherwise we won't be able to use it once Simon is fully awake, if there's an emergency. Neither can we keep on giving him a sleeping draught," said Beth.

"You're right," replied Mike, running his fingers through his hair. "We really need to think about moving him out of the attic."

Once they had moved the trunk, Jake took an old chair into the smaller room, to sit and wait for Simon to wake up.

Beth, carrying the tray, entered the kitchen by the side door. "Thanks for the tray, cook, Mike did appreciate it."

"Good," cook replied. "I don't know how you managed to hide the little lad and then return him to the attic, maybe it's best I don't know. I do think we should move him to Jacob's house on the quay, down in Torrington, as soon as the visitors have gone."

"You think Jacob will be willing to help him?" asked Beth.

"Yes and Simon will be safe there."

"When are the visitors leaving?" said Beth.

"About 12.30pm, after an early lunch. How is the boy now?" queried Cook, as she continued to work. "Is he strong enough to walk down to Torrington or do we need the bath-chair?"

"I think he can walk, if we take it easy. He really needs to put on weight and rest up for a while longer, but he is coughing less."

"I'll make him a fried egg sandwich and a mug of tea, if you want to take it up to him," said cook. "Tell Mike to pop in to see me, if he's still hungry."

"You'd best make it two sandwiches, Jake's with him," said Beth, with a grin.

When Beth returned from the attic, she told cook both boys were delighted with the sandwiches as she noted cook's look of concern.

“You know,” said cook, “I could not bear to think of Simon maybe ending up in the workhouse, not after what I saw there. Thank you, for helping the lad. Between us, we will keep him safe,” she confided. “Oh and I spoke to Wilkins. He was sure Mr Mandeville would be happy to give Simon a job, but that it was best to leave it a while, until we know Mr Grimshaw has definitely gone. No point in risking him finding out that Simon is here and maybe stealing him away, once more.”

“I’m sure that he would not recognise him, now he’s washed and wearing those clothes. He looks quite smart,” replied Beth.

“Once we have fattened him up, he won’t be able to fit up a chimney,” laughed cook.

---

## Chapter 18

### Flying High

Mike, Robbie and Pete left the main house loaded down with several valises and swung them up onto the wagon. John and Thomas made for the stables. Mike, on hearing the horses whinny, turned to see them being brought out. They were led by their reins and tied up to the front gates. They all gave a hand to give the stables a final clear out. The straw and muck was added to the compost heap at the end of the garden.

Once their chores were done they joined Lewis and Mr Mandeville a little while before lunch was due to be served. When Beth joined the gathering, she whispered to Mike that Simon was being moved later on to Jacob's house and that he might even have a job in a few weeks' time. Mike gave her a broad smile.

Lunch over, the horses were hitched to the wagon ready for the off. The young men said their goodbyes and each in turn gave Beth a peck on the cheek. Thomas also gave her a hug.

Beth felt her face hot, as she blushed. She stood with cook, Wilkins, Lewis and Mr Mandeville, to wave goodbye, as Mike and Thomas walked behind the wagon in procession, as it set off along the cliff top road. Beth slipped away to the attic to let Jake out, knowing he would be eager to see the balloon being launched. Simon was sitting in his smart second hand clothes and his hair shone a light golden brown. He had been stretching his legs, by walking up and down the room with Jake and they had managed to bundle up the spare clothes Mike had purchased, along with the nightshirt, ready for Simon to take with him. Beth explained the plan before Jake hurried off, making for the field near the church, to meet up with the others.

It was an hour later and the day had turned warm but overcast. Cook was carrying a basket and Beth carried a parcel of clothes tucked under her arm, as they headed down to Torrington. Simon was between them holding on to their arms.

Jacob was happy to take the boy in, saying he would be glad of the company. Cook handed him a stock of food and Beth the bundle of clothes.

“Well, now lad, you may call me granddad, while you’re here. Is that alright with you? And you will be sleeping in the parlour?”

“Thank you, Sir.” replied Simon

“Granddad,” Jacob reminded him and Simon smiled.

“I never knew my granddad,” said Simon, beginning to come out of his shell.

“That’s a pity,” said Jacob, obviously taking a liking to the lad, “I never see my grandchildren, as they live many miles away. We will do well together,” he said, reassuringly.

Cook gave him a big smile. “I shall visit when I can. Now I need to get back. Afternoon tea will be needed soon and I have left it all ready to be served." Beth noticed that Jacob gave cook a quick peck on the cheek and that she blushed. With that Beth and cook began their journey back to Wattle Peak.

***

Once the wagon, with its cargo and the deflated balloon, reached its destination, Mike watched as they set about inflating it once more. Long bursts of hot air slowly filled the canopy. Quite a crowd stood staring in awe. When the job was half done, Mike decided it was time he found the Reverend Barclay. He came upon him, just as he emerged from the vicarage and Mike quickly explained how they had rescued Simon.

"I guessed something had been going on," said the vicar, "after Mr Grimshaw visited me and made such a scene accusing me of helping you to take Simon from him. I sent him on his way with a flea in his ear. Mrs Grant told me this morning, that he has now left the village, sneaking away last night, owing money at the Inn, so he daren't show his face there again."

Mike grinned, "We have Simon safe and there is the likelihood of a job for him at Wattle Peak, when he's well again. However, my reason for seeking you out was to ask a big favour," said Mike. "I have been promised a ride in the balloon, as far as Hayle, but only if I have transport back."

"I see, so you need a lift. Well, after your generous donation for those clothes, I think I could give you that and I, too, want to see the balloon in action. Indeed, I need to visit Simon's mother at the pottery, it's not far from Hayle. I fear she must be worried about him if Grimshaw visited her yesterday. So how about we meet at the north end of Hayle town later this afternoon for the return journey?"

"Oh thank you, that would be wonderful," said Mike gratefully and hurried off to let Thomas know that he could now join them for the flight.

Mike met Jake on the way and explained about his lift.

"Do you think I could go with the vicar for the ride and meet up with you later," suggested Jake.

"Why don't you go and ask him now?" Mike replied and watched Jake scamper off on his mission.

At 1.30pm. the balloon was nearly ready for the off and a crowd milled around eagerly. Jake and the vicar sat in a pony and trap ready to follow the wagon for most of the way.

Watched by the crowd, Mike made his way up the steps, before lowering himself into the balloon basket. He realised that he was a little apprehensive after the problems Beth had had with her flight but never-the-less he found it very exciting. Soon the balloon lifted slowly into the air, to cheers from the crowds on the ground. Mike drank in the fascinating sight of the whole of the village laid out below him and Wattle Peak in the distance, as they made their way north by northeast.

***

Jake had watched anxiously, until the balloon was safely on its way. Then the vicar called ‘giddy up’ and off they in the pony and trap following the wagon. The flight had gone without a hitch. When they reached the crossroads, just few miles before the road that led down the hill to Hayle, Mike returned Jake’s wave as there they parted company. Jake and the vicar took the turning towards the potteries. They shouted their goodbyes to the lads in the wagon who continued on to Hayle following the balloon. Mike had a grand view of the potteries, with their tall chimneys in the distance and the roads leading to it with hovels nearby, where the workers shuffled to and fro.

Jake and the vicar moved swiftly along, the rump of the light brown pony moving rhythmically in front of them. The orchards they passed were heavy with fruit, pears, apples and plums all nearly ready for picking. So were the blackberries in the hedgerows, where other berries partly red and seeds of all sorts were ripening.

“Simon is being taken to Torrington this afternoon,” Jake explained.

"Humm…" replied the vicar, "it might not be wise to tell Mrs Jamison exactly where he is for the moment, safer that way."

"I asked Simon this morning, while helping him to get dressed, how things were when he worked for Mr Grimshaw and what he said had made me very sad."

"Go on, what did he say?" asked the vicar.

"Simon said that he was never given enough to eat, as Grimshaw wanted to keep him skinny, otherwise he would not fit into some of the smaller chimneys. The only clothes he had were the ones his mother had given him 18 months before and since then he had grown two inches in height. There had been holes in the knees and elbows of his clothes, so he had no protection from the rough bricks when startled by birds and he slipped, or a brick gave way. He spoke of how, each night, Grimshaw had made him soak his knees and elbows in a basin of salt water to toughen the skin and how that caused his grazes and broken skin to smart. He said, that on one occasion, he had suffered a broken rib and that Grimshaw had strapped strips of old cloth tightly around his chest, before sending him back to work the next day, even though he was crying with the pain. His master had told him that the pain would remind him to be more careful in future."

"One day, that man will get his just desserts of that I'm sure," said the Reverend Barclay angrily.

Jake continued, "Simon even tried running away, after he was beaten for eating the food given to him by a kindly cook, at one of the houses. After that, when not working, Grimshaw kept him on the end of a rope and locked him up at night whenever possible. He hated going into those dark narrow openings, with his brush on a string around his neck and was scared when he climbed out onto the steep roof, to make his way to the next chimney, to climb down once more. The soot got into his eyes and also made him cough."

"It's so wicked and now you can see why it was outlawed," said the vicar, "but it might be best not to tell Mrs Jamison, how much her Simon has suffered. I fear she will already be regretting her decision to move to the potteries, although she had only been trying to do the best for her family."

As luck would have it, Mrs Jamison had just finished her shift and on seeing the Reverend Barclay, who she knew by sight, she began to tremble fearing that he had come to give her bad news of her missing son. She anxiously made her way towards him.

"You're the Reverend Barclay from Pennington are you not?" she said, her voice shaking.

"Yes and you are Mrs Jamison?" queried the Reverend, drawing the woman away from listening ears. As she nodded her head her eyes began to fill with tears. She had dust in her once golden hair, her dress was ragged and she had a shawl tied about her. She walked slightly stooped from carrying heavy loads.

“It’s alright, Mrs Jamison, I haven’t come to tell you bad news,” said the Reverend kindly. On hearing this, the woman’s eyes brightened and she looked at him, with hope.

“Has he been found?” she asked.

“Well yes, with the help of my friend here.”

“Oh thank you,” she said, turning to Jake.

“However, you mustn’t let on that Simon is safe, if asked, say you still don’t know where he is. You see, we need to make sure Grimshaw has left the area, before we can bring your son out of hiding, as Grimshaw may have friends listening out for news. We will tell you at a later date where he is. All you need to know now is that he is getting better and is being well looked after.”

“Better you say,” she said, clutching his arm.

“Yes. Well, he had a bad chest infection but after all the care he received, he will be fine. He must never again work where there is fine dust.”

“Oh, I’m grateful, sir,” she said, with a smile.

“It’s not me you should thank but several others who wish to remain anonymous. Anyway how are things with you and the family?”

“Oh sir, the work is so hard especially for the younger ones. The rent here is high and what with paying Mrs Wicken, to look after my babies, we have to work all hours just to survive. The children all have coughs due to the dry clay dust. Their jobs are to carry bricks or move the dry pots, before they are glazed and fired in the kiln, and the dust can be very bad.”

"I'm sorry to hear that," said the vicar, "I know you came here to find a better life. I shall come and see you again in a month or so with more news. I was asked to give you these," He handed her two sixpenny pieces, which were a gift from Jake.

"Please, thank them for me," she cried, closing her hand tightly over the coins.

The vicar then noted down where she lived before waving goodbye.

Jake looked around as they made their way back to the trap. He saw people going into the potteries, pulling scarves around their mouths and noses to protect them from the dust.

***

Aware the evening was drawing in, they hurried off to meet Mike, who was waiting for them on the outskirts of Hayle. While journeying towards Wattle Peak once more, a beaming Mike, full of excitement about the flight, entertained them with all the things he'd seen and particularly about the landing which had been very bumpy. "I'm sure I have a few bruises to prove it," he chuckled.

"There you are," said Beth, pleased to see them back and to know that Mike was safe and sound. They waved the vicar goodbye and turned into the grounds of Wattle Peak. "Well, we really must set off for home. It was time to go and say goodbye to Lewis and his grandfather."

They explained to the Mandevilles that they would be away for a while with their parents and unlikely to be back before the last week in October. Lewis was sad that he wouldn't see them for some time, so Beth promised him she would bring Sooty with them on their next visit.

Beth hoped their plans for Simon would work out, but knew she'd have to wait many weeks before discovering, if all had turned out well.

---

## Chapter 19

### Victorian Election

It was late October and half term at last. It had been a busy start to the new school year and they had all had to get used to their new form teachers as they had moved up a year. At the beginning of the half term week they had enjoyed a few days out with their parents, but by Thursday they were impatient to head to their attic for another visit to the past.

It all seemed very quiet as they emerged from the tack room into Victorian times, but there was a smell of horse dung, which made them wonder who might be around. They popped into the kitchen to see cook and find out what had been happening.

"Hello," said cook, as she gave Jake a hug and smiled at the other two. "Lewis and Simon will be disappointed to have missed you all. They have gone to Hayle in the new pony and trap."

"So Simon is staying here now, I'm so pleased," said Beth.

"Yes, Mr Mandeville was happy to have him here, especially after the Reverend Barclay called and told how the child had been treated. He also told him about Simon's family's problems. The boys now spend all their spare time together. Simon is such a good worker. He's in charge of the pony and will take over driving the pony and trap from Wilkins in due course."

"Oh, what a shame we missed them. We will be around all day, so we will come in again on our way back."

As they headed into the village, they remembered about the election. The contestants and the ballot sheet would be in The Square there for a few hours, before setting off for one of the other polling stations.

On entering The Square they saw a stage had been set up. Posters were hung around this platform, where two men sat. One was the local squire, a rather large red-faced man dressed in a tweed suit and the other a thin short man dressed all in black.

Outside the King's Head stood a trestle table set up with beer and cider for sale. They could see men with tankards of ale milling around. Some appeared quite drunk although it was only eleven o'clock. In a side road, the hiring fair was well under way, men, women, young girls and boys, stood lined up with their bundles.

They made their way to the stalls, where Jake found his old favourite, honey and almond cakes. Beth made for the stall selling sheepskin rugs to find out their prices then she made a note of where the pasties were on sale. If the boys agreed she might take a rug back for their attic as they were so lovely and soft.

Beth walked around the square. She stopped at the milliners shop and saw a cream hat that would go well with her present outfit and go even better with her summer outfit which, as the days were now quite cool, she had put away. She was wearing the wine dress with a cream shawl, rather than the heavier cape and on realising that her current hat really did look rather out of date, she entered the milliners to make her purchase.

***

Mike had bought some lemonade and was standing with Sooty, waiting for the others. He had been watching the election proceedings for some time and had noticed money changing hands. Some rough-looking men were handing out silver florins and buying drinks, but they did not look the sort who could afford to give away their money. He then realised that someone else was doling out the money to these men. The donor stood half-hidden behind a high sided cart. Mike moved further round the square so he could see who it was and saw a man in his forties dressed in a smart dark green jacket. The leather bag from which the man produced several coins appeared to be empty. He delved in and rooted around inside and finally, carefully, turned the empty bag inside out. Mike watched, as the man made a beeline for the Squire, on the other side of the square. He whispered in the squire's ear and the squire handed him another bag - so the men were all working for him concluded Mike!

As Mike made his way back, an angry man in a brown jacket was telling the squire's men to get lost. He didn't want their money and he would vote for who he pleased. Then, as the man tried to move away, the two of them grabbed him and dragged him down an alley. Mike heard the man cry out in protest. Sooty, barking loudly, ran after them. "Oh, Lord," cried Mike and chased after Sooty on hearing several thuds as the two men kicked their hostage, as he lay curled up on the ground. The victim's agonising cries horrified Mike. Sooty launched himself at one of the assailants' legs and yelped when the man kicked him. Mike was too late to stop Sooty as he got up and launched himself back into the fray.

"Hoy there," shouted Mike, brandishing his walking cane at them. The two men quickly made off when they realised, that, with Mike and the dog, they were now out-numbered. Having heard Sooty yelp, Jake ran to help and arrived as Mike placed his arm around the man's waist and assisted him to his feet. Jake began to brush down the man's now dusty coat and the dust made him start to cough.

"Thank you all for your help," said the man, who was clearly shaken and patted Sooty's head, as the little dog came and reached up to him. They all headed back towards the Square. They found a bench to sit on and Mike opened the lemonade, offering it to the man who gratefully took a drink.

"What was all that about?" asked Jake.

"I told those villains I wouldn't vote for the squire, that's what, so they offered me a bribe. When I said I wouldn't want to see a man like that get into Parliament and certainly not with my help they set about me. They wanted to make sure I didn't vote for anyone else, so it was just as well you came along when you did."

"We were pleased to help," replied Mike.

"Did you know the squire owns one of the potteries and brickworks where children work for 15 hours a day? He knows the powdery clay gets into their lungs but he doesn't care. He and his like are out to block the coming reforms that are needed to restrict children and women working in bleaching, dyeing and lace-making works. With luck, the reforms should be passed in the next 12 months. The squire is afraid that, if these new measures are passed, then the potteries will be the next to be brought into line and that's the last thing he would want."

"Let's hope it all goes through," said Mike.

"My name is Gerald Black by the way," said the man.

***

When Beth joined them they were deep in conversation. Mike stopped speaking to introduce their new friend. "Gerald Black this is my sister Beth," said Mike, with pride.

"Mr Black owns a small farm and orchards a few miles away," explained Jake, "and he was set upon by the squire's men, until Sooty came to his rescue."

"Why would they do that?" asked Beth, as she handed out the hot pasties she was carrying. She had even brought one for Sooty, but offered it to Gerald, who gratefully accepted. They sat devouring the savoury pastry, with their chunks of swede, turnips, potatoes and meat, breaking off bits for Sooty as Gerald replied.

"It's the usual story, if you won't toe the line and vote for the squire, they try to stop you from actually voting. The squire has created temporary tenancies for many of the people in his pay, so they can claim the right to vote. Bribery and corruption they call it. However, I must be off to vote as the ballot closes at 2pm."

"How will they know who you voted for?" asked Mike. "They won't see your ballot paper as you put it in the box."

"Ballot paper you say, that's a new one on me. No lad, you have to tell the electoral official who you are voting for and he writes your name on the candidate's ballot sheet which is taken from one polling station to the next. What you are talking about is a secret ballot which is part of the aims of the Chartist movement. They hope to get the vote for all men over 25 years old. I'm one of the lucky ones, as I own a property worth over £10 so I already have the right to vote. There are a few other ways you can qualify but not if you are poor or don't own property. Did you know that only one in six men can vote or so it was reported in the 'The Cornish Times.'?"

"We will go over to the voting table with you to prevent anyone else trying to get to you, while you vote," suggested Mike.

"No, thank you kindly, you may find yourselves in trouble if seen with me, so you had better not. I shall be alright now, thank you. After I've voted and done my errands, I'll come back and find you, if that's alright?"

"Yes, do," said Beth, who laughingly added, "we will keep watch from here and send Sooty in to help, if needs be."

A little later, they saw Mr Black coming towards them, carrying toffee apples. "I was hoping I would find you," he said smiling. "I got these for you they may even have been made with my own apples."

"Thank you. How did the election go?" asked Mike, taking his apple.

"Oh, it is not over yet, it takes two days for the voting, but from what I saw of the voting sheet, the squire has most of the votes. His opponent, Brother Watson, a Methodist lay minister and a supporter of votes for all men, had very few votes, I'm afraid. It's only what I expected. Too many people's livelihoods around here depend on how well they get on with the squire."

"It will change one day, I'm sure," said Mike, sounding positive.

"It may not be for many years yet but hopefully I shall see it in my lifetime," said Mr Black. "Well, I must be off now. It was nice to have met you all. Call in, if you are near my farm,

Orchard Grove. It's on the road to Hayle, about 4 miles from here and you might like to try my cider." With that, Mr Black went off to find his horse. He waved from his chestnut cob, as he passed by them, a little later.

The Reverend Barclay spotted them in the square. "Come to see the voting?" he asked. The children told him about Gerald Black and how he was attacked. "That doesn't surprise me, I'm sorry to say. Gerald is a good man, who recently lost his wife and struggles to bring up his two young children. Oh, I know you will be pleased to hear that Grimshaw was seen boarding a boat in Hayle, bound for south Wales."

"That's wonderful news," said Beth.

"So Simon can breathe easy, if you will excuse the pun," said the vicar, with a grin. "He is doing fine at Wattle Peak and I understand he is company for young Lewis."

"On our way back, we are hoping to see him and Lewis," replied Mike.

The children headed back towards Wattle Peak. As they drew close to the Georgian house they heard a pony and trap behind them. They turned and waited.

Simon jumped out and rang the bell that Wilkins had rigged up, so that it would ring in the farmhouse kitchen, warning the caretaker that he was needed. A second door had been added to the farmhouse kitchen, so the caretaker could leave that way, to open the gate from inside the grounds. As he emerged, Beth thought the caretaker seemed very much older than when they had first seen him. He walked much slower.

The children gratefully accepted Lewis's invitation to afternoon tea. While Lewis and the boys joined Mr Mandeville in the drawing room, Beth made for the kitchen, to arrange for tea to be served. Simon and Wilkins were still busy looking after the pony.

Cook had just taken a batch of buns out of the oven and the smell was heavenly. Beth helped prepare the large tea tray, as she told cook all about their adventures in the Square and of their meeting with Gerald. "Did you know Grimshaw had left the area?" asked Beth.

"Oh yes, that's why it's safe for Simon to be out and about again."

"How is he settling with the caretaker?" queried Beth.

"Things are alright, but with the caretaker's hearing being so poor, he's not such good company for the lad, as Jacob was, I'm sorry to say."

"And how is Jacob?"

"He's missing the lad. He had grown really fond of him."

"The old caretaker seems to be having trouble walking," commented Beth.

"Yes, I fear his days here are numbered, but I understand that his sister, who lives in Torrington, is keen for him to move in with her. So we may be looking for a new caretaker soon." Just then Wilkins arrived to pick up the tray.

Simon sat with Lewis on the drawing room floor, taking turns at rolling a ball for Sooty to chase. Wilkins set down the tray. Mike had just finished telling Mr Mandeville about the voting. Beth handed around the napkins and tea plates for the buttered buns.

It gets dark much earlier now, thought Beth, so it would soon be time for her and her brothers to leave, before the sun actually set, fearing that perhaps Mr Mandeville would insist on Wilkins driving them home.

The sun had started it's descent as they left by the front door. They passed the farmhouse and moved outside the small gate, there to linger a while before daring to return to the attic. They stood watching the sun getting lower and lower, as the bright yellow sky turned pink and orange, then faded into twilight. It was then, as the light dimmed, that they returned via the side gate, moving silently up the stairs, wondering about their next trip and realised there were now only a few visits left.

---

# Chapter 20

## Simon's Family

Next morning, a bleary eyed Beth made her way to Mike's bedroom and tried to stifle a huge yawn as she entered.

"What's up with you?" he asked, on seeing her dishevelled state, "you look, as mum would say 'like you have been pulled through a hedge backwards'."

"No sleep, that's what. I have been going over and over it in my mind for most of the night, the problems of Simon's family, the Jamisons. You know what the vicar told us, a while back, about their plans."

"I do remember some of it, but why are you so worried?"

"Oh Mike, Simon can no longer work in any sandy, fine dust or smoke environments because of his weak chest caused by working in those dreadful chimneys, so there's no way he can work with them at the potteries. His family planned to get the babies back when Simon was able to join them in a year or so and then they would all work together. Simon, being there to help, and by doing the shift work, they could have looked after the little ones between them until they, too, could work but that can no longer happen. It just doesn't seem fair after all Simon went through. Though it certainly wouldn't do the little ones health any good working at the potteries."

“Yes, you’re right. How about we have a word with the Reverend Barclay, when we next visit and see if anything can be done? I hate to see you upset,” replied Mike. “He might know of some work for the family. Try not to worry Beth.”

“By the way, what were you talking to Mr Mandeville about before we left?”

“Oh, just an idea it may come to nothing. It was something cook said to me about the caretaker, that he might be leaving to live with his sister.”

The Halloween disco party and the following weeks’ firework night celebrations, with its huge bonfire, were great fun, the perfect way to brighten up the dark winter nights. They were looking forward to Christmas but that was many weeks away, so they decided they would venture back in time again in three weeks’ time.

It was a Saturday morning, four weeks before Christmas, when they set off for the farmhouse attic there to swiftly change into their Victorian winter clothes, in the cold rooms. They emerged, quietly and cautiously from the tack room, before hurriedly leaving the grounds by the small gate. They moved quickly along the cliff top road making for the vicarage to seek out the Reverend Barclay. There was a chilly wind coming off the sea but the sky was a brilliant blue. It was not long before they saw the vicarage and as they walked towards the house they watched the blackbirds attack the berries on the ivy clad garden wall. On reaching the front door Beth pulled on the bell chain.

"Hello, Mrs. Grant, is the vicar in?" she asked.

The housekeeper smiled at her weakly, "Unfortunately, he isn't, my dears," she replied, shaking her head and wringing her hands, in a worried fashion.

"What's wrong Mrs Grant?"

"Do come in, my dears," she said, before leading them through to the parlour.

She turned to look at them. "You remember Mrs Jamison, Simon's mother, who left her twins with that child minder, Mrs Wicken?"

"Yes, we do, so what is the matter?" queried Mike

"Well, this morning, while in the general stores, I heard Mrs Wicken's maid-of-all-work, tell the shop owner's wife, that her mistress was expecting a windfall, as a couple from Exeter were coming that afternoon to pick up twins. The couple had been searching for many months for blonde twin boys and were willing to pay well."

"How many twins does Mrs Wicken look after?" asked Beth, suddenly concerned.

"That's just it, Miss Beth, as far as I know, there's just the one set, Mrs Jamison's boys!"

"She can't do that!" said Jake alarmed.

"What can we do to stop her?" asked Mike.

"We must go and get Mrs Jamison from the potteries, so she can rescue the babes," pronounced Beth.

Just then, they heard the door open and with relief they saw the Reverend Barclay.

“Well now,” said the Reverend, on hearing the news, “I think Beth is right, we must go and get Mrs. Jamison and find out if she knows anything about this matter. I’m sure she hasn’t agreed to it.Would you like to come with me Beth?” he continued, "there is room for four in my cart.”

“Yes, please,” she replied and they went outside to where the vicar had just left it, the boys following.

“What can we do to help?” queried Mike, ‘and how long do you think you’ll be?”

“There is something you can do, Mike,” replied the Reverend Barclay. “Do you know the lane leading up to the child minder’s home? It’s close to the tin mine; Water Lane they call it.”

“I’m not sure, but we will find it,” he replied.

“Go there and keep watch, so you can tell me if the couple have arrived. It will take us three hours to get to Mrs. Jamison’s and back. ”With a wave, the two set off.

Mike noted that according to the church clock, it was 11am as Mrs. Grant called to Jake and Mike and asked what they were going to do. When she realised how long a wait the boys would have, she told them that if they held on a while, she would make them a sandwich to take with them.

Luckily, though a November day, it had remained sunny and once they were away from the sea breeze it wasn’t too cold and even quite pleasant as they set off to find the address.

When they met the road leading to the mine they turned right away from the mine and eventually, saw a lane leading off the road on their left. As a stream ran along the side of the lane, Mike reasoned it must be Water Lane. They made their way along it until they saw a large house and a sign stating 'Wicken House'.

There the maid was busy pegging washing on the line, so quietly the boys made their way back down the lane. The house appeared to have been part of what had once been a large estate, as all sorts of fine trees, including pine, had been planted along the lane. After lunch they were beginning to get bored, so with Christmas in mind, they decided to collect some pine cones, then selecting the best from what was beginning to become quite a pile. They placed them in the bags that had contained their sandwiches.

It was then that Mike, who was closest to the mine road, heard a pony and trap approaching. He moved out into the road to see if it was the vicar indicating to Jake to stay out of sight. Sitting inside the trap were a smartly dressed middle aged man and a woman. The man caught sight of Mike and called out "Hey, Boy, you there! Can you tell us the way to Mrs. Wicken's house?"

"Mrs Wicken's house? I believe it's on the other side of the mine," Mike replied, "Go up this road, go past the mine and you should see a road on your left. If you take that road and keep going, you should see a big sign to her house."

“Thank you,” said the woman and they moved off towards the mine.

“What did they want?” asked Jake, when Mike returned to their hiding place.

“The way to Mrs Wicken’s,” he replied, with a chuckle, “so I have sent them on a wild goose chase. They should end up back in the village.”

“That was a good idea, Mike.”

“They will be back in a short while, so let’s hope the vicar arrives here soon,” added Mike.

As they walked back to the road, they spotted the vicar’s familiar pony and trap. Beth and Mrs. Jamison were with him. When told what had happened, the vicar instructed the boys to stay where they were and keep out of sight, but to run and warn him if they saw the couple returning.

Mike stayed by the road but Jake disappeared in the direction of the house as the vicar’s conveyance made its way up the lane. All three alighted, leaving the carriage behind the hedge and entered the front garden of a huge house with its large windows, where the blinds were drawn at the front. There were no children running around, everything appearing unusually quiet. As Mrs Jamison rang the doorbell, the other two stood back a little way out of sight. The maid opened the door a fraction and on seeing Mrs. Jamison, snapped rudely,

"What do you want? You know it's not your day for visiting and Mrs. Wicken doesn't like her routine disrupted."

"I need to see her right away, please tell her I'm here."

"She may not be at home," said the maid, closing the door, only to return shortly after. "She can't see you now. Come back next week, at your appointed time. Now, be off or else!" On saying this, she closed the door with a bang.

Despairingly, Mrs Jamison looked over to where, unseen by the maid, the vicar and Beth were stood. He quietly called Mrs Jamison over and patted her hand, as she started to cry, then told her to go back to the pony and trap and keep out of sight. He had needed to witness, for himself, the way women who came to see their children, were really treated. Mrs Wicken, always seeming so nice when he had called on her in the past.

The vicar strode over to the door with Beth and he sharply rang the bell, the maid opened the door a few minutes later.

"You asked for it," she yelled, as she threw a bowl of water over the vicar, drenching him. As a look of horror appeared on both of their faces, the maid mumbled, "Oh no! I'm so sorry Reverend Barclay, I did not realise it was you at the door, I thought it was that tramp back again. Oh, please come in, I'll fetch a towel."

As he entered the hall, the vicar shook his head to remove some of the water, Beth following behind him trying not to laugh. The maid returned with a towel, the vicar scowled at her and stated he wished to see her mistress. Having asked them to wait and looking very scared, the maid headed off down the very long corridor. They slowly followed her, hearing raised voices in the distance. Beth quickly opened each door as they passed before quickly closing it again. She stopped when she saw what she had been looking for and entered the room to have a closer look at two cots. Inside these she found two identical blonde children, sleeping, both appearing clean and quite nicely dressed. They had name tags pinned to them, identifying them as William and Freddie. 'Bingo!' whispered Beth to herself, and returned to the corridor, just as Mrs Wicken emerged from the end room and came bustling along to meet them, very concerned at what her maid had done.

"Do come into the office," she said, charmingly, "so sorry for the mix up. The maid is bringing tea. Oh, is this a young lady wanting to use my services? You are lucky, my dear, I happen to have a couple of vacancies. Please sit down, do."

"No she isn't, Mrs. Wicken," said Reverend Barclay, "sorry to disappoint you, but we're here about Mrs Jamison's twins, as she is anxious to have them back."

"Really, well now, that does surprise me, considering she owes me a large sum of money and hasn't visited here for six months. Has she now found the money?"

"I believe you are mistaken about her owing you money, Mrs Wicken. Indeed, if you check your records, you will find all is in order, for she's told me herself that she's been here every month and paid you what you asked."

"Oh dear, oh dear, you really can't believe a word her sort say. She knew the rules and signed an agreement. I do have to protect my business or this place would have to close down and you tell me, where would all those mothers who have need of my services be then?"

"Mrs Wicken, I really must insist you check your records. I believe you do her a grave injustice."

"Really, has she shown you the receipts for the money I received from her then?"

"Why no, she hasn't."

"Of course not, because she hasn't paid me for such a long time. When she first started to miss payments, she just kept promising she would make them up. That happened month after month, then nothing. I saw neither hide nor hair of her for the last few months, then out of the blue, she turns up wanting them back! Naturally, I considered that those children had been abandoned, so gave them up for adoption, some weeks ago."

"But, surely," interrupted Beth.

"No, leave this to me please," said the vicar.

He let Mrs Wicken continue. "You may not know this, but I only ask the new parents to refund me the monies owing and a small donation, if possible. I assure you, they went to a good home. I always do what is best for the children."

"Be that as it may," replied the vicar, "yet surely…"

"Come, come," interrupted Mrs Wicken, "let us waste no more time, the deed is done, so there is nothing more to be said. Now, if you will excuse me, I must get on." At which point she looked at her watch and rose from her seat, signalling them with her hand towards the door.

'She's desperate to get rid of us,' thought Beth, 'as the couple wanting the children would be there soon.'

Reluctantly they rose to make their way outside. The maid walked closely behind them, then she hurried to open wide the front door for them. "Good day, sir, miss," she said, as she closed the door.

Beth was bewildered, but waited until they were out of earshot before saying anything. "This is all wrong. We only have her word for what she told us," she said furiously.

"Calm down, Beth," said the vicar, "I have to speak to Mrs Jamison about what that woman said."

Mrs. Jamison was sitting in the trap hidden by the tall hedge. There were tears in her eyes. "Did you see my babies, tell me, when I can have them?" she pleaded.

"It seems we are too late," he replied solemnly.

"Oh no, no!" cried Mrs Jamison, desperately. "How can she do what she likes with my children?"

"Did you sign an agreement with her?"

"Yes."

"Do you have a copy?" asked the vicar hopefully.

"No."

"Can you remember what it said?"

"Oh, Reverend, I can't read," she said, sobbing.

"Oh, Lord," said the vicar, in silent prayer. "What about receipts for the money you paid?"

"I had no receipts. She entered the amount in a big book and I made my mark next to it."

"Please," said Beth, impatiently, "are your children called William and Freddie?"

"Why yes, how did you know that?"

"They are in the third room on the right," said Beth, beaming, "the woman is a liar, you can't trust a word she says. I did try to tell you, vicar."

"Are you sure?" said the vicar, astounded.

"They even had their names pinned on to them," replied Beth.

"Mrs. Jamison, was the book you mention red?" asked Jake, who had come out of hiding and been standing there listening.

"Yes, red with a black border down one edge."

"Then I know where it can be found. When you all arrived, I went to the back of the house and found the office. I stood listening by the open window. When she knew you were there, I heard her telling the maid she had to get rid of you as soon as possible and once the maid left the room, I peered in the window. Mrs Wicken was panicking. She walked round and round the room, looking for somewhere to hide that book. She eventually decided to put it under the drawer section of a desk - the one with short legs."

"Well done, young man, but how do we get hold of it?" said Reverend Barclay.

Just then Mike came running up the lane, "They're here!" he said, out of breath "and I had better hide, in case they might recognize me."

As the couple climbed out of the trap they nodded to them all and made their way towards the front door. Once again, Jake headed around the back.

The maid answered the door, curtsied and was heard to say, "Good afternoon sir, madam. The mistress is waiting for you in the parlour, where tea will be served in just a few minutes." She took the gentleman's hat and coat.

Mrs Wicken was heard introducing herself to the couple as they made their way towards the parlour.

Jake hurried back, carrying the red book and handed it to the vicar who, taking a quick glance at the entries let out a sigh of relief. "Thank goodness," he said, "we've got the evidence here that you paid her, these entries confirm it. Jake, can you get back in there again and open the front door? You will have to be very careful though, so as not to bump into the maid." Jake nodded and off he went once more.

***

Jake climbed in through the awkward, open office window and crept around the desk, only to hear Mrs Wicken open the parlour door, saying she would just get the paperwork from the office. To his horror, he heard her footsteps on the wooden floor, as she hurried in his direction.

Jake, wide eyed with fear, held his breath, as she opened the door wide. When she let go of the handle, he pulled the door towards him, standing nervously behind it. He heard her making for her desk to retrieve the essential forms, then grabbing the door handle once again to pull it to. Relief flooded through him, as he heard the noise of her footsteps diminishing, as she headed back to her guests. Jake let out a silent sigh, waited a minute, before he checked the long hall. Having taken off his shoes, he silently made his way to the front door and opened it. Mrs Jamison and Beth hurried along and into the room, where Beth knew the youngsters were and carried them back towards the open door. Once outside, Jake closed the door, which unfortunately made a loud clunk, so they ran towards the pony and trap which was still behind the hedge. Once safely out of sight, Beth peered through the hedge and saw the maid open the front door to check the garden, but on seeing nothing amiss, shrugged and went back inside.

As the carriage only held four, the boys decided to head off to Wattle Peak and disappeared into the woods, out of sight. As quietly as was possible, the Reverend Barclay led the pony and trap a short way down the lane, before he got in. Mrs. Jamison's eyes brimmed with tears, as she looked at her two year - old sons, William in her arms and Freddie cradled by Beth. Both children had been unnaturally quiet, so they feared they must have been drugged.

The pony and trap swiftly headed off to the main road towards Hayle. Worried, Beth asked the vicar, “What will happen when they realise the babes have gone? They will have guessed where they are and may even threaten Mrs Jamison.”

“You leave all that to me to sort out, Beth,” assured the vicar, “we have that book, don’t forget, also I have a plan - just you wait and see.”

---

## Chapter 21

### Orchard Grove

The pony and trap continued on for several miles before turning into a side lane, riding alongside a large orchard for several minutes, until a farmhouse with a large barn came into view, where they stopped. On seeing its name, 'Orchard Grove Farm,' something stirred in Beth's mind, as she alighted from the carriage to open and then securely close the gate, once the cart finally stood in the farmyard. The geese in their pen set up an almighty din. Gerald Black, along with his sheep dog Bess, swiftly emerged from his barn on hearing the commotion, to see what was amiss.

The dog went to over to investigate sniffing and wagging her tail, as Beth helped Mrs Jamison, struggling to get down from the trap, while holding her son in one arm. The Reverend Barclay steadied the horse. Gerald beamed at Beth, as he went over to shake the vicar's hand.

"Hello, Gerald," said the Reverend, "you may remember our discussion regarding Mrs Jamison and her family, well, I have her with me today."

"Of course I remember," replied Gerald and turned to Mrs. Jamison. "I'm very pleased to meet you and I see you have brought your youngest with you," he said, whilst admiring the two sleeping babies.

"We have a problem, Gerald," said the Reverend Barclay.

"Where are my manners?" exclaimed Gerald, "please come over to the house and have some tea while you explain."

The house was very old, quite large and made of wattle and daub, like the farmhouse at Wattle Peak. Rose bushes surrounded the door and under the windows. Chickens scattered every which way across the yard as the group made their way to the front door.

They entered a large warm kitchen and sat down at its long table, as a kettle was gently steaming on the range.

"Tell me, what brings you here today?" queried Gerald, as Beth helped with the tea things. Mrs Jamison handed Beth the sleeping baby and poured out tea for them all.

"Well, Gerald, today we had to steal these two youngsters away from Mrs Wicken's premises as she was about to sell them." Gerald's mouth dropped open in shock and he almost choked on his tea, as the vicar explained at length just what had been happening.

"I'm afraid I haven't yet explained to Mrs Jamison your kind offer to take her and her children into your home, in return for looking after your house and your children, and her own youngsters helping you to run the farm. It's very generous of you. I'm sorry to have to ask you to bring the plan forward."

"Its fine, I'm sure we can manage," said Gerald, running his fingers through his hair.

Mrs Jamison looked at them both, as her eyes filled with tears. “You would do that for me?” she said, almost in a whisper.

“I need help and with luck, we may be able to manage without any of your children having to go out to work elsewhere. Can’t promise any wages I’m afraid, but if all goes well, then sometime in the future, that may be possible. In the meantime you will be well fed, have a warm home and a roof over your heads. Furthermore, any money you or your family can earn in their free time, will be theirs to keep. Are you willing to give it a go?” he added smiling, “your name is Martha, I believe, is that right?”

“Yes, sir,” she replied, lowering her eyes.

“Gerald please. We will be working in partnership and this will be your home.”

“It all sounds so wonderful, but where are your own children?”

“Oh, Rosie the scullery maid has taken them down to the river and should be back shortly. She is only eleven years old and has been finding it hard, trying to help me look after them, since my wife died. I have neglected my work in the orchard and the cider making, so I could do with the assistance of your lad and daughter.”

“I see. I’m sure Barry and Lisa would be happy to work here and maybe, even Simon one day.”

“I think,” said the Reverend Barclay, breaking in on their discussion, “you need to go and get your children, Martha, from the Potteries, just in case Mrs Wicken takes her anger out on them. She might have gone after the babes, claiming that you still owe her money, unaware as yet, that we have her book. Also, I do need to get Beth back to her home."

"Right," said Gerald, "let's get moving. Beth, would you go and get two bottom drawers out of the chest of drawers from the upstairs bedrooms; they will be the largest ones. Leave their contents on the beds for now and bring them down here, together with a couple of blankets from the deep chest on the landing. They will make temporary cots for the babes. I had all sorts of plans, but as there has been no warning, I have not had time to open up the loft as another bedroom, or to make a few more beds, so we will have to make do."

"Have you any bottles we can use, for the little ones when they wake?" asked Martha. "I doubt somehow that Mrs Wicken would have weaned them off the bottle yet, that's why they are so small for their age."

"Try that wall cupboard, there may be some old ones in there and there's milk out in the dairy. I own two cows," replied Gerald.

"It would be best to leave them ready, just in case the little ones wake, while we are out," Martha added.

"While you are doing that the Reverend and I will hitch up my cart," said Gerald. "We will set off as soon as possible. if Beth and the vicar are willing to wait here until Rosie arrives back with my two? My Jimmy is four and Jenny six and half," he added proudly as he turned to Martha.

Soon they were waving Gerald and Martha off and returned to the kitchen. "While we are waiting, we could peel some potatoes," said the vicar, "after all there will be quite a few mouths to feed tonight." So both set to work and filled a very large pot.

When Rosie arrived back, she was surprised to see two strangers busy in her master's kitchen and in the process of clearing up.

"Those peelings need to go in the pig swill bucket under the sink," said Rosie, noticing that Beth was at a loss as to what to do with them. Suddenly, Rosie and Gerald's two youngsters saw the babies and crowded round to have a look. "Where did they come from?" asked Rosie in a daze.

"Well, not from under a gooseberry bush," chuckled the vicar.

Beth and the Reverend quickly explained what had been happening and that they needed to go. "Martha and Gerald will be back very soon with two more children, so there will be quite a few to be fed tonight, no doubt you'll have some other supplies to add to the potatoes. We will have to leave you to it," said Beth.

"Will you tell Gerald, for me, that I will keep the red book safe?" said the vicar, "he will know what that means," Rosie nodded.

Beth took off her the apron she had donned and she told Rosie about the bottles needing warming, if Freddie or William should wake. She then quickly put on her cape.

Rosie waved them goodbye and as it would soon be sunset, they set off at a smart pace, knowing it unwise to travel after dark. Beth shivering sat huddled against the wind in the pony and trap.

An hour later the vicar dropped Beth outside Wattle Peak and turned the cart around ready for home. "Thank you Beth and thank your brothers for me," he said, "I know just what to do with the book," and grinning, he waved goodbye.

Beth crept quietly up to the attic to find her brothers waiting patiently to hear all the news. They had already eaten half the cake cook had given them to take home. The Mandevilles were out for the day and the boys entered the attic before they were likely to arrive home. It was only then that Beth realised how hungry she was and in the nearly dark attic tucked into a slice of cake

"It's time for home," said Mike, having heard all about Orchard Grove Farm.

"Only two visits left," said Jake, with a sigh.

"I'm afraid so," replied Beth, as they crowded around the trunk and as Mike opened the lid, the room whirled, taking them home once more.

---

## Chapter 22

### Christmas Presents

In the middle of December Beth, Mike and Jake dressed in their Victorian clothes and headed into the bygone era. The air had a nip to it as they wandered up the path, Sooty stayed by their side barking excitedly. Jake carried a brown paper parcel under his arm.

Both Lewis and Simon nearly bowled them over at the big front door of the Georgian house, when they came rushing out to greet them. Simon squealed with delight as Sooty licked his face. The young lad now appeared fit and well, thought Beth.

"Come in, do," said Wilkins, shivering by the door. "It's perishing cold today and we are letting all the warm air out." They hurried in and took off their capes, handing them to Wilkins, "Mr Mandeville is in the day room," said Wilkins, "he will be pleased to see you all."

Lewis's grandfather sat by the large Adam fireplace, his face quite rosy from the heat of the fire.

"Hello," he said brightly, sitting up in his large winged armchair, "I'm pleased you have called early today or you would have missed us. The coach will arrive shortly to take us into Hayle for the Grand Saturday Market, the last before Christmas. Would you like to come?"

"Oh, yes please," replied Mike happily, the others enthusiastically agreeing.

"I need to buy a few things as Christmas presents for my granddaughters. If I send them now, they will arrive at their hotel, in Paris, in time for their visit there on Christmas Eve. Perhaps you, Beth, would help me choose their presents? We might also spot a few other things for Lewis and Simon."

"Oh, I would love that."

"Good, the coach will be here in half an hour."

Simon and Lewis asked if they might come too, but Mr Mandeville told them that might spoil their Christmas surprises. As both boys looked glum, Jake stepped forward, "I have brought with me just the thing for a cold winter's day and he untied the parcel, to reveal a chess board along with chess men and draughts pieces."

"I have always been fond of a game of draughts or chess," Wilkins said, "I'll be pleased to show both Simon and Lewis how to play." Their faces brightened, as Jake took them to find a small table to set up by the fire and explained the rules of draughts. The younger boys were absorbed by their new game when Mr Mandeville found them to say goodbye. "Now remember, Wilkins is in charge while I'm out and you must do as he tells you."

Mike returned to the hall to find the bath chair, so it was ready for loading on to the coach. On hearing the coach arrive, Wilkins appeared with their capes and a few blankets, as the coach could be quite cold. He made sure Mr Mandeville was well wrapped up against the cold, as they left the hall. Once they were all safely installed in the coach and the bath chair secured on the roof, Wilkins tucked the blanket around his master, "do tell cook we will be back for a late lunch at say 2.30pm. I fear it will be too cold for me to stay out any later." said Mr Mandeville.

As they travelled along, Mike asked for the latest news of the happenings in Pennington. Mr Mandeville chuckled. "Oh, what a hornet's nest you've all stirred up, by helping the vicar and Simon's mother, to rescue those babes from that dreadful Wicken woman." His face suddenly became serious. "That was a bad business and many women have come forward, since the vicar published the details in the Cornwall Times. As a result, the police have built a case against her."

"We would love to see the newspaper," said Beth, "have you kept a copy?"

"Yes, I thought you might. I doubted it would appear in Exeter's newspapers. Wasn't that where you were staying?"

"Yes, that's right and no, we didn't see anything about it," said Jake, agog at the news.

"Where was I… oh yes, the police were too late to arrest her; she managed to escape. She'd tried to get the rest of her rent money back from the landlord, as the lease had another year to run. However, he refused and made her relinquish the lease, in return for not demanding, that she carried out any repair work that might be needed."

“Good for him,” said Mike.

“Later, when he heard what had been going on at his property, he was appalled. He told the vicar that if he could find someone to take over the business, he would let them have it, rent free, for a year, thereby allowing them to get the business going again.”

“That’s wonderful,” said Beth, as she thought of all the mothers who needed their babies minded, if they were to make a living.

“The Reverend Barclay has roped me in as one of the directors, would you believe.”

“That is really good news,” she replied, “I know you will see it’s run properly.”

“Certainly, I will. Oh, you must pop in and speak to cook when we get back, she has some news too. I promised I would ask you to go and see her, when you next called.”

Having already passed the turning leading to Gerald’s farm, they were soon turning off down towards Hayle, which had grown considerably, since they visited in Georgian times. The road was crowded with people heading for the market, so progress slowed to a crawl.

Once the coach driver found a good place to wait, they helped Mr Mandeville into his chair. “Hold tight to your purses,” he reminded them. Beth had her purse around her waist, on a belt under her coat. She told the boys she had brought enough money for them to buy presents for their parents and for their friends at Wattle Peak and doled out the coins.

When they arrived at the jeweller's shop, Sooty was let off his lead to stretch his legs and to follow close to Mike's, who was hoping to buy Sooty a new collar, as a Christmas present. The boys went off in search of various presents that were to be given from the three of them.

The jeweller's shop was full of watches, grandfather clocks and jewellery of all kinds. "Well, Beth, any idea what I can buy for two young ladies, aged fifteen and seventeen?"

"What about jewellery boxes?" Beth suggested.

"I'm sure they already have them, as they would have needed them, while travelling."

"Oh, these are beautiful," said Beth, looking admiringly at some blue-green opals. Within each stone, the fire of different colours flashed as they were moved - yellows, pinks and orange, appearing deep within. There were others, some of a milky cream background with many colours that flickered in the light and gleamed at each turn.

"They are from Australia," said the jeweller, "a new find."

"Which do you like the best, Beth?" asked Mr Mandeville.

"Maybe those with a deep blue-green background, it's such a pretty shade." The jeweller brought out a tray for them to examine. After some negotiation, a price was agreed for two pendants with gold chains. These purchases were, put into boxes, wrapped up and tied with gold ribbons.

"Now, what may I buy for you and your brothers as presents? You have been such a help with Lewis," said Mr Mandeville, waving his hand towards watches and jewellery.

"That is very kind of you, but I am sure our parents would not appreciate someone they'd never met, buying us presents." Beth had realised it would be hard for them to explain to their parents any expensive gifts. "There is something you could help us with," she said, "and that would be very much appreciated, as we don't think we have quite enough to buy one outright. It is something I saw back in Pennington."

***

Mike meantime, fought his way through crowds of people of all types, from the rich to the very poor. He shivered, when he saw the ragged children in threadbare clothes, gawking at the many fine things on display. The noisy calls from the many traders were quite deafening, as they tried to outdo each other. He eventually came upon a stall that sold sheepskins. He picked out two rugs, one for each side of their parent's bed, and after much haggling, agreed a price. While the stall keeper was wrapping them up, he spotted a sheepskin blanket and bought it, along with a pair of sheepskin slippers, the latter for Beth, a present from himself and Jake. He then went off to the leather stall, to find the right size collar for Sooty.

Mike found the stall he wanted and the belts took his eye. He picked out a few as presents and a purse for mum. He then turned to the dog collars, but when he looked around for Sooty to try one on him, he was nowhere to be seen. “Oh, no, where is he?” Panic set in, as he hurried back the way he had come, calling for the dog and hoping to find Jake.

***

Jake had found a stall selling plum puddings and bought a large one for his family to share and a very small one for himself. He also bought a fancy box of honeycomb for Beth and some honey and almond biscuits in a tin, for Mike, hoping he would get a share.

What could he buy cook, he wondered? Then he saw the very thing, a book stand to hold her recipe book open and he also found a silver pen for Wilkins.

Jake had stopped to buy some chocolate and had passed close to where the animals were kept for sale. Standing near to these, was a man who opened a sack and took out a black dog and held it up, not unlike Sooty thought Jake, as the man shouted, “Dog for sale, who will give me two shillings for this guard dog, house trained and good with young’uns?” The man looked shifty and had on hobnailed boots, brown trousers and a rather tatty jacket. Jake shrugged and moved on.

***

Beth wheeled the bath-chair into a bookshop and there she chose some books for Lewis and Simon, as presents from herself and her brothers. She reached up to a shelf and found a few blank books for them to draw or write in. 'Wrapping paper, colourful string and sealing wax,' she said to herself," realising she needed to wrap up some of their presents and leave them ready for Christmas Day at Wattle Peak.

Mr Mandeville suggested tea, so they sat in a pleasant tea shop, close to the market, out of the cold air. Delicious cakes surrounded them and they found it hard to choose one as they all looked so good. Beth found her mouth watered dreadfully. Canisters of teas were stacked on shelves all around ready for purchase. So many varieties, thought Beth.

"When will your son and family arrive at Wattle Peak?" Beth asked.

"As they were delayed in setting off for Paris, they won't arrive back here until early in the New Year.

"What about you, what are you doing at Christmas, will you be in Torrington? Perhaps you could bring your parents to meet us? We would love to see you all," he added.

"I'm afraid not. We will be in Exeter until just before New Year's Eve. We will be back at our Aunt's, for a day or two, to pack up a few things before setting off for London on New Year's Day. A coach will pick us up early and we will meet up with our parents in Exeter. They are going to a New Year's Eve ball, with friends there."

"Well, you must come and say goodbye on New Year's Eve, promise?"

"Of course we will," she said smiling.

***

Mike found Jake as he stood looking at the sweet stall, "Have you seen Sooty, I can't find him anywhere?"

"Oh, no," said Jake. "I saw a man trying to sell a dog, I thought the dog looked a lot like Sooty, but his collar was gone. Quick this way." They pushed their way through the crowds to where the man was still trying to sell the dog.

"Stop that's my dog," shouted Mike, as the man was about to close a deal.

"Don't talk rot," the man replied, "he's mine! go away before I clout you one," and he raised his fist.

"Give me back my dog. Jake, go and fetch a policeman," shouted Mike. Jake moved quickly off into the crowd. The man who wanted to buy the dog looked worried and stopped counting out his money.

"If you don't go away now, I'll give you a black eye, you lying little toe rag. Take no notice of him, Sir, it's a nice little dog, my children loved him and will miss him sorely, but needs must."

Jake searched around desperately for a policeman and wondered what else he could do. He didn't want Mike to be hurt. The piercing sound of a whistle rang out and Mike heard Jake yelling. "This way officer, the thief is over there," as he pushed his way through the crowd. At the sound of the whistle the man had dropped the dog and took to his heels. Mike called to Sooty, who ran whimpering into his arms.

"Where's the policeman?" asked Mike. Jake grinning, took from behind his back his penny whistle and gave it another blow for good measure, "that should keep him running." Jake laughed, knowing that police blew a whistle to attract other officers and to warn people to get out of their way, when chasing a villain.

"Well done, little brother. I don't think we should mention this to anyone," said Mike. At that, Jake grinned.

"You might be right, otherwise I would have to listen to Beth telling you off all the way home."

"Too right, you would, I'll carry Sooty until I put a new collar on him and can attach his lead. Can you take a few of my parcels for me?"

"Sure, see you back at the coach," said Jake and hurried off.

***

It was time they were all back at the coach; Beth and Mr Mandeville had just settled themselves in the carriage. The driver had stowed the bath-chair away as Jake arrived back and placed his purchases in the box hanging on the back of the coach, before taking his seat. He opened his slab of chocolate and shared it with them. They were munching away, when Mike and Sooty arrived.

"I have just seen Gerald; he has a stall selling his cider and apples. He told me all is working out well at the farm. He has introduced a few more pigs and they will be allowed to roam in the orchard, in the spring and summer. It was Mrs Jamison's idea. She had seen this done on a farm when she was a girl. The pigs ate the fallen apples and kept the ground clear before the crop was ready for picking."

"Did you get everything we needed?" Beth asked him, as she watched him putting a sack of goods into the coach's box, before climbing into the carriage.

"Of course I did," he replied, pushing Sooty inside. The coach set off and Beth wrapped one blanket around Mr Mandeville and another around herself. Although it had been very cold so far there hadn't been any snow.

Back at Wattle Peak, a fine lunch had been prepared; a warming broth to start with and game pie to follow. "The apple crumble was delicious and the custard just right, thick and creamy," remarked Jake, as he finished it off.

Mike agreed to start wrapping up the presents in the study, so the others wouldn't see what they were while Jake kept the youngsters entertained. Mr Mandeville returned to the day room, to sit by the fire and have a short nap.

"There you are, Beth," called cook, as she entered the warm kitchen. Cook had been busy washing up the dishes and after quickly drying her hands she gave Beth a big hug and thanked her for her help.

"Help?" said Beth blushing.

"Come on, Beth, I know it was you who spoke to Mr Mandeville about Jacob being the next caretaker here."

"Oh good, I'm so pleased, but really I only mentioned that Simon and he got on well and Jacob was a very good friend of yours."

"Well, he starts here straight after Christmas and as he knows about horses he'll be able to teach Simon all he needs to know. Once Mr Mandeville's son and family arrive, there will be at least one carriage kept here and a pair of horses as well as the pony and trap.

"Gerald's scullery maid will be joining me here, as I shall need help, what with the Mandeville family and the mistress's lady's maid to cater for and look after. The place will be buzzing."

Beth was very pleased with herself as she made her way back to see how Mike had got on with wrapping the presents. She helped him with writing the labels, signing the gifts from all three of them. She liked the sheep skin blanket for Mr Mandeville and helped Mike wrap it up.

Beth told Mike about the jeweller's and how she had diverted the money Mr Mandeville would have spent on them, towards a present for the Jamison family. This meant the cost of the sewing machine was paid in full, instead of the family having to pay off the balance in due course, when Mrs Jamison made a profit from using it.

"It was a good idea of yours to buy the sheepskin rugs for mum and dad, instead of buying one for ourselves," said Beth.

"Yes, you're not the only one who has good ideas. I've also arranged a special gift for Simon and Lewis."

"Oh, what is it? I have already bought them some books."

"You will have to wait and see." said Mike maddeningly.

"I'll go and find Jake it's time we made for home. Mum knows we were going shopping but the shops at home will be closed by now. We also need to say our goodbyes and sort out which parcels are ours to take home."

"Don't forget Sooty."

"As if I would," she replied and hurried off.

Ten minutes later they had finished wishing everyone a Happy Christmas and promised to be back on New Year's Eve. Juggling the parcels in their arms, they waved farewell and headed for the small gate. Shivering, they waited outside in the biting cold wind that blew straight into their faces. When all was quiet, they re-entered through the gate and hurried into the farmhouse attic. Huddled around the trunk, Beth lifted its lid, and off they went to their own time once more.

"Just one more visit," said Mike, as they moved towards their front door, carrying their parcels. Sooty plodded slowly behind.

"What has Mr Mandeville bought Lewis and Simon for Christmas?" asked Jake.

"I don't know, but he was very mysterious about it," replied Beth.

---

## Chapter 23

### Ringing Out the Old

To their delight their parents were thrilled by their Christmas presents of sheep skin rugs and the other gifts they had brought back from the past. Beth was particularly pleased with her slippers from Mike and Jake. She had bought her brothers cinema tickets, so they could go to see a special showing of the film ‘Star Wars Episode V–The Empire Strikes Back’ both having missed it on its release They would travel to see it with a few of their friends, along with one or two of the dads.

Beth loved the party dress from her parents, which she chose all on her own, while her brothers received money to buy tickets for a pop concert in addition to some music cassettes and books.

On New Year’s Eve their parents had a party of their own to go to and as they were helping friends to set it up, they would be leaving home early.

“Make sure you lock up when you leave for the disco,” instructed their mother as she was about to leave with their father, “and that you’re home by 12.30. Have a good time and make sure you stick together when returning home.”

"Yes, mum," they chorused with a sigh and watched them leave.

The children quickly made for the attic for their last trip into the past. It was true they were off to a New Year's party, but not the one their parents assumed. Beth had spruced up their Victorian clothes with an iron and handed the boys gold cufflinks and cravat pins from the jewellery box, found in the trunk. For herself, she had laid out a necklace with a ruby drop. She also had ready the shell pink blouse made of heavy satin to go with the wine coloured skirt. She had saved it for a special occasion and ironed it carefully, along with the matching pink shawl.

Mike found he was looking forward to Mr Mandeville's party at Wattle Peak, even though it meant missing the disco with his friends. Jake was particularly looking forward to the special treats cook would be making.

It was early evening, about six o'clock, when they arrived for the final visit in 1860. They made their way to the big front door with its holly wreath threaded with red and gold ribbons. The candlelight shone from the windows onto the frosty ground, making it glisten and Sooty left a trail of small footprints, as he wandered around the front garden, sniffing excitedly with his tail wagging furiously.

Flares had already been set up in the front garden to light up the drive-way for the guests who were due later.

It was Mr. Mandeville who had suggested they arrive early so they would have time to talk with Lewis, Simon and the others about their Christmas activities.

Beth gathered her brothers to her and said solemnly, "It's important we leave this era before the clock finishes striking midnight, or we might be stuck here forever. So remember, at ten minutes to midnight we really must leave. Got it!"

"Aye, aye captain," said Jake, saluting Beth.

"Beth's right, so stop taking the mickey," replied Mike, seriously.

"Oh, but we will miss all the fun as the New Year is rung in," said Jake sullenly.

"Sorry, Jake but that just can't be helped," said Mike.

Beth pulled the bell and Wilkins opened the door and smiled, "Happy New Year," the three chorused loudly.

"Happy New Year to you all," he replied cheerfully, as he stood aside for them to enter. "Mr Mandeville has almost finishing dressing. Many thanks for the pen it was most thoughtful of you all. Oh, by the way, Simon and Lewis are with Jacob, in the farmhouse."

"Of course, he is the caretaker now," replied Beth.

"That's not all," said Wilkins, grinning, "you really should go through to what is now the ballroom and have a look. Sounds very grand doesn't it. We have opened the partitions to make one large room out of the day room and drawing room. It still has all the Christmas decorations and with both fires lit, it's quite warm in there."

The boys quickly removed their capes and Beth hers to reveal her pretty pink top and silk shawl, that made her look quite grown up, as her ruby necklace sparkled in the candlelight.

"You will have to excuse me, as I must get on, there is still much to do," said Wilkins, as he whisked away their cloaks and disappeared.

They found the ballroom quite inviting after the frosty night air. They stopped as they entered the room, surprised by the sight of the huge Christmas tree with its ribbons, tinsel, edible striped candy walking sticks and many small candles, making it all so very pretty. Nearby, stood two large gold painted buckets filled with water.

Jake looked puzzled, "In case of fire," whispered Mike, "remember, there's no fire brigade nearby to come to your aid after a swift phone call. Didn't you notice that in the cupboard under the stairs there were dozens of buckets of sand or water?" Jake shook his head.

So far, only a few of the wall candles had been lit, making the large room seem almost cosy in the glow of firelight. Sooty curled up by the fireside, gave a yawn and promptly went to sleep.

"I'll go and give Wilkins a hand, lighting the candles," said Mike, "all those candles will take forever, what with the chandeliers and extra candelabras needed. Jake disappeared in the direction of the dining room to see what had been put out for supper. Beth followed them out heading for the kitchen to see cook.

Cook was about to pour a cup of tea as she saw Beth poke her head round the door. Beth noticed a twinkle in cook's eye and her beaming smile. "Beth, my love, you did remember to come and see me. You know, I shall miss you all when you leave, come, join me for a cuppa." Beth noticed the table was absolutely full of the dishes of food for tonight's buffet and they looked wonderful.

"Yes please," replied Beth, "it looks like you have finished all the food."

"Yes, only have the plates and bowls to sort, ready to go on the sideboard in the extended dining room.

"Did you like our present, the bookstand and the new book for writing recipes in?"

"Oh yes, a lovely gift and I'm sure 'my Jacob' will want to thank you all for his cravat."

Cook was excited about something, thought Beth. Of course, she had just said 'My Jacob'. "No, you didn't, did you? 'Your Jacob' you said." Beth squealed with delight, as cook showed her her wedding ring and gave her a big hug.

"Yes, we didn't want a lot of fuss, so we tied the knot at the Christmas Day church service by special wedding licence. It was a surprise to all, except Mr Mandeville, as we told him beforehand and the Reverend Barclay of course."

"That's lovely news, are you living in the farmhouse?"

"Yes, Jacob will let out his cottage on the quay and put the money away for our eventual retirement. When Jacob finishes making Simon a bed, he will sleep in the attic and part of the attic will be curtained off, for use as a school room for Lewis, Simon and Rosie the new maid. Mr Mandeville is determined his staff will all be able to read."

"That's good news, but where are Lewis and Simon? They are usually out to see us, like a shot, when they know Sooty is with us."

"Oh, didn't Mike tell you about the boys' Christmas gifts, the ones they got from Gerald?"

"No, he didn't tell me what they were."

"Well, I'll not spoil the young ones pleasure in showing you," said cook, finishing her tea and clearing away their crockery. "They're over with Jacob in the farmhouse at the moment. Why not pop across and see them? Take your brothers with you, there's time before the first guests arrive."

"Thanks cook. I'll let you tell Jake your good news, when we get back."

Beth found Mike lighting the last candle. "Cook has suggested we go over to see Lewis and Simon, they're with Jacob in the farmhouse. Something to do with a gift via Gerald that you arranged?" queried Beth, still puzzled as to what it could be.

"Great. Let's find Jake. If he wasn't in the kitchen with you then he's bound to still be in the dining room." Sure enough, there he was, busily re-arranging a few small cakes on a stand, with tell-tale crumbs around his mouth.

"Oh Jake, couldn't you have waited a while longer?" said Beth, as she shook her head at him. "Come on, glutton, we are going over to the farmhouse for a few minutes."

They dashed across the drive and garden in the cold night air and knocked at the door. Jacob opened it. There, sitting at the table were Lewis and Simon, each holding the most adorable puppy, one being black, the other a mixture of white and black.

"Oh, they are beautiful," said Beth, stroking the baby soft fur. "Are they collies?"

"Part collie," replied Jacob. "Gerald wasn't sure who fathered Bess's litter, but a cross breed is often a less demanding dog than a thorough-bred, so easier to manage. Collies need to be kept occupied all the time, if they are not working dogs."

Simon smiled brightly, looking up at Beth and her brothers, "Oh, thank you, for arranging these. Would you mind if I called mine Jake?" he said.

"I'll call mine, Mike?" added Lewis, "that way we won't forget you all, when you leave."

"That would be lovely," said Beth and her brothers nodded, rather pleased by the idea, but had looked sad as they heard the words 'when you leave.'

"Time to put them back in the basket by the range," said Jacob, while putting down some newspaper on the floor, as the pups were not yet fully house trained. "Simon, you will need to help me open the gates shortly and a little later to light the flares around the drive, plus the two outside by the roadway, so they are ready when the guests arrive."

"We will see you later," said Beth, giving Jacob a peck on the cheek. "Congratulations by the way," she whispered, while the boys made their way out.

"I see you have spoken to Rachel," he chuckled. "Once I got the job here, I got up the courage to ask her to marry me."

"I never knew that was her name, it's a very pretty name. I know you will be happy. We will see you later at the party."

Wilkins had finished setting out the last of the chairs in the ballroom. The local fiddle players and the ballad singer had arrived. "Gerald, along with Mrs Jamison and her two elder children, should be here shortly," explained Wilkins, as he inspected the room with Beth by his side. "Rosie, their scullery maid and her friend will be looking after the younger children this evening, including little Freddie and William. Tomorrow, Rosie will arrive here to 'live in', as our house maid and her help will be most welcome, what with all the clearing up to do."

"That sounds good. What about the Reverend Barclay and Mrs Grant, we were hoping to say goodbye to them?"

"Yes, they will be here. Gerald will bring them in his cart, along with some of his best cider."

"Is there anyone else coming?"

"Oh yes, but a little later, at about eight o'clock, well after all your friends have arrived. There will be the ladies from the dress and milliners shops, along with several other trades people and their youngsters, among others"

"Quite a crowd," said Mike, having caught most of what was said as he entered the room.

They moved back to the dining room, away from the fiddlers, who were tuning up, as a smiling Jake came to join them. "Did you hear about cook and Jacob?" he asked.

"Yes, wasn't that good news?" said Beth. The doorbell was heard and Wilkins headed off to greet their friends.

"I just left Mr Mandeville in the ballroom," Mike explained, "he's in his bath-chair, so that he may be moved around amongst his various guests."

"I'll go and make sure he is comfortable," said Beth.

"Hello Beth," said Mr Mandeville as she entered the ballroom, "how lovely you look my dear. I can see that in a few years' time you will be quite a heartbreaker with your good looks." Beth felt herself blush a deep shade of pink.

“Oh, I see you have the sheep skin blanket we bought you.”

“Yes, a very welcome gift. Now, I think I heard the bell, so hopefully that will be some of your friends. I invited some guests early, so you would have time to see them all, before it gets too busy.”

“That was kind of you, it would be nice to see and chat with them for a final time and to say goodbye properly,” said Beth, her eyes beginning to fill with tears.

“Now, now, my dear, don’t be sad. We will be sorry to see you all go but you never know, you may come back one day and it has been good while you’ve been here.”

She turned away and wiped her eyes. Through her tears, she saw Gerald, Martha Jamison and her two eldest, along with the Reverend Barclay, walk into the room. After greeting Mr Mandeville, Mrs Jamison thanked Beth, her brothers and Mr Mandeville for the sewing machine, “Such a wonderful gift.”

Beth moved away with Martha and Lisa to hear how they were getting to grips with the machine. Beth explained that her grandmother had one with a foot treadle, on which she had made cushion covers. She remembered the problem she had, spinning the wheel by hand, to get it going the right way, just as you started the treadle.

“There is still work like hems and button-holes to be done by hand,” said Lisa, “I can help with them until I’m able to use the machine.”

“When I enquired about the sewing machine,” said Beth, “the ladies in the milliners and dress shop, told me that they were looking for someone to do alterations to some of the clothes their customers bought and requested that I let you know."

"Oh, that would be good," said Mrs Jamison, smiling at her daughter."

With Mike in tow, the Reverend Barclay pushed Mr Mandeville in his bath-chair across the room to where Gerald warmed his hands by the fire. Sooty stood up and gave a big stretch then settled by Mike.

"I hope you have given Simon and Lewis some good advice about training their dogs," said the Reverend on seeing how well Sooty was behaving.

"Yes, I gave Lewis a list of instructions and I know Gerald will help, which was part of the deal," chuckled Mike, "after all we can't have them getting under Mr Mandeville's feet."

"The puppies almost outshone the gift I bought them," said Mr Mandeville.

"Oh, yes. What was it you got for them?" queried Mike.

"Well, I sent off to Scotland, to a Mr Kirkpatrick MacMillan, for his most recent model of the bicycle. I gave him the boys' heights and he has made them accordingly. They are much better than the types made solely of wood that you propel along using your feet, though those do work quite well and were certainly much quicker than walking. The new bicycles are really very special and are in the stables, if you and Jake would like to see them?"

"We have used bicycles," said Jake, on entering the room.

"Yes, we tried them in Exeter" said Mike. Beth saw Mike turning to give Jake a warning look in case he said too much. "It takes a while to get the hang of it but once you find your balance you're fine though I would like to see these latest versions, wouldn't you Barry?" added Mike. Simon's brother, Barry, appeared rather shy, but nodded and followed Mike and Jake eagerly as they went outside.

As the boys disappeared, Beth sat down with her friends, to ask about their plans and about their Christmas festivities. The fiddlers were playing softly in the background as drinks were handed around. All of a sudden the drive came into life as all the flaming torches were lit. Everyone moved to the tall windows, as they heard the squeals of laughter from Simon and Lewis.

Mike and Barry helped to hold upright Lewis's bike and Jacob and Jake held up Simon's, as the boys tried to ride the bikes round and round the drive. Each of them wobbled dreadfully when they tried it solo. Luckily, they were quickly caught before they fell over. Shortly after, the first carriage arrived bringing the other guests and the bikes were put away. Everyone had enjoyed the children's fun.

"What did you think of the bikes, Mike?" asked Beth, when she got him on his own.

"They have wooden frames, but metal pedals that actually turn the wheels. They are a great step forward, but the wheels only have solid metal rims and the ride is quite uncomfortable, as you can feel every bump and stone in the road."

"So you wouldn't swop it for your mountain bike then?" she chuckled.

"No way," he whispered, "but they will find them better when used on the new road surfaces laid on the main roads when they visit Gerald."

Soon the party was underway, with the fiddlers playing a lively tune and the guests dancing. Even Jake took to the floor with Lisa and she laughed as he stepped clumsily on her feet so as she patiently showed him the dance steps.

Once the buffet was ready everyone filled their plates and returned to the ballroom. A hush came over the room as several beautiful ballads were sung with everyone joining in the chorus as they ate their food. Mr Mandeville announced a toast before the dancing recommenced. "To Rachel and Jacob congratulations on your marriage."

A little speech followed from the Reverend Barclay thanking Beth, Mike and Jake for the things they had done during their stay. He wished them a safe journey and good luck for the future on their return to London with their parents. Everyone cheered and clapped. Beth went to kiss him and thanked him for his kindness and help during their visits, then he whisked her away for the next dance.

It was very warm as the dancing got underway once more. Beth looked around the room with its elegant glowing candlelit tree. The laughter and happy atmosphere seem to give the scene a magic all of its own. A wonderful evening, she thought, knowing the image would stay with her forever. Mike kept a wary eye on the grandfather clock in the hall, remembering Beth's words, as midnight approached.

Beth knew the fiddlers would very soon be tuning up for the singing of 'Auld Lang Syne', as she and the boys, sadly, said their final farewells. They stood in the doorway together, looking around at all their friends for the very last time. As they left the room to slip quietly away they could not see Sooty.

Mike went to collect their capes. "Jacob, have you seen Sooty?" he asked.

"Oh, yes, he is in the farmhouse with the puppies."

Beth, anxiously, turned to Mike, who was putting on his cape and he handed Beth hers, "Oh, where's Jake?" she said, beginning to panic, "he was here a moment ago."

"It's gone five minutes to midnight, we are cutting it fine," stated Mike, looking at the grandfather clock.

"I don't know where he is. I warned him about this," said Beth frowning.

"I'm just going to collect Sooty from the farmhouse," said Mike, "I'll put him on his lead and at least we will know where he is. I'll meet you in the attic. Here, take Jake's cape."

"Right," said Beth, putting the cape over her arm. "I'll check the dining room and then the kitchen. If he's not there, I'll assume he's already in the attic with you." Both moved off swiftly, too afraid to even think of the consequences, if they did not find Jake before midnight.

Beth searched the dining room, even lifting the tablecloths to check under the tables and from there she moved quickly into the kitchen, across the hall, but there still was no sign of Jake. She checked in the pantry in case he was in there. Desperate, she made her way out to the front door, pausing only to check the main room once again. The grandfather clock's hands moved, to one minute to go and still no trace of Jake.

People were beginning to form a circle for the singing of 'Auld Lang Syne', as she raced across the yard, into the tack room. Puffing and clutching Jake's cape, whilst trying to hold up her cumbersome skirts, she climbed the steep stairs, finally reaching the top step. The room was semi dark with only the moonlight to illuminate it, just as the countdown began - 'six, five, four..., Beth's mouth dropped open, Mike was alone, Jake was not there... shouts of 'Happy New Year' rang out and the cheering started.

Beth went to stand closer to Mike, on whose deathly pale face there was a look of horror. He clutched Sooty even closer and grabbed Beth's hand, "We still have each other, Sis." He looked sad and his shoulders drooped. "What will our parents think, when they never... see us again," his voice trailed off to a whisper.

"Oh, no, don't say that Mike. Jake, what have you done?" Beth cried in despair, tears beginning to fill her eyes.

Then they heard the tack room door open and Jake bounded up the stairs.

"What's up with you two?" he asked, seeing their gloomy faces, "I know I'm a bit late," he added contritely, looking at his pocket watch, "but we still have two minutes to go." They looked at him, bewildered. "Oh, don't tell me you didn't check your watch, Mike? I put all the clocks and the big grandfather clock forward by five minutes, so we could enjoy the excitement of the count down," he said, biting his bottom lip, trying to hide a grin.

Beth gave a huge sigh and closed her eyes briefly. "Trust you to do something so daft," she said.

"Get, over, here," cried Mike, through gritted teeth. Relieved, he held on to Jake as Beth lifted the lid of the trunk and the room whirled for the final time.

As they looked around their attic, they were all sad, having seen their friends for the last time. Beth would have liked to have stayed mad at Jake but it was not her way. Jake had grown up a lot in the last few years and she found he was good company, but at times, as nutty as ever.

They were quiet as they changed into their own clothes, agreeing to leave putting the Victorian clothes away until later and it was only then, as Mike put on his own watch, he realised it was only 10.30pm in their own era. "We still have time to join our friends from school, at the disco, if we get a move on."

“A second New Year party in the same evening,” replied Beth, as she followed Jake out of the attic.

“Race you back to the house,” said Jake, as he sped off, with the twins following close behind and Sooty keeping pace with them.

“You won’t take long getting ready, Beth?” pleaded Mike, “or we will miss all the fun.”

“As if I would,” said Beth, with a grin, “ten minutes, if you’re lucky, I’ll meet you in the hall.”

A little later, the three linked arms, as they made their way along the cliff top road, until they met the smaller road that lead to the church, with its new hall. The moon was full and shone brightly on the frosty path, as they walked along, remembering how this path had been on their first adventure and how it had changed over their various visits to the past.

They could hear the pop music playing in the distance. The party was in full swing and should be fun. However, of the two parties, it would be the Victorian New Year’s party, that would stand out in their memories, of that they all agreed, as they hurried along, happy once more.

---

## Chapter 24

### Remembrances

It was a cloudy day in February, when Henry's Cousin Warren and his son Alan called to have tea. Alan was now on good terms with Mike and Jake, ever since he joined their school and started playing sports with them. The tea party had gone really well.

"I'm eager to know what you found in the other two trunks." stated Warren.

"The second trunk we opened contained items relating to Georgian times and the last Victorian," said Mary, as she proudly handed around the pictures of them in the Victorian costumes. Even Alan began to take an interest.

"As you know, the first one related to Cromwell's era," added Henry. "The second had items from the Georgian period 1760 or there about and the third from the Victorian era."

Henry and Warren chattered about days when they, as youngsters, spent time in the Georgian house and how it looked back then, with its old conservatory. They reminisced about seeing it pulled down, as it needed too much work to repair it. "Not really so surprising, it had been up since mid-Victorian times," remarked Warren.

"I still think it was a great pity it wasn't saved," muttered Henry.

Warren produced a parcel that contained a book and handed it to Henry, "It belonged to our Aunt Anna, a sort of journal I'd say, anyway, something for the family archives. It tells of a journey she made to the West Indies, to the island of Jamaica. She had a bee in her bonnet about tracing some relative from Georgian times, a James Pendleton, I believe. You may be able to trace him in the family tree."

"Really, I'll enjoy reading it," said Henry, gently opening the book. "Thank you."

"There are also two letters dated 1763 and 1764 from James Pendleton, sent to a local school umm… St. Joseph's School and Home for Children, apparently she found them with some old records, which had been kept with the church archives."

The three children looked at each other in surprise, excited at the thought of reading her journal and Jamie's letters. Their father promised to let them read them, as soon as he had finished with them.

After tea, the boys and Beth took Alan over to the attic and opened the Victorian trunk to show him some of the contents. He particularly liked the top hats and canes, as they took turns to saunter around with them, making up jokes.

"Waiting a few more days won't hurt," said Mike, when Beth complained the following day at having to wait to see the journal. "Why don't we go down to the churchyard and see if we can spot the graves of any of those we met in the past? It's not so cold today."

Wrapped up warm they headed for St George's Church. Unfortunately, some of the really old grave stones were badly weathered and couldn't be read. The name Pendleton just about visible on a few, but the first names and dates eluded them.

In the section to the left of the church, were the Georgian graves and there they found Lucinda Wainscroft, Great Uncle Jamie's fiancée and the other victims of cholera - the scourge of that era. She was such a lovely young woman, thought Beth. "Oh, there's Captain Watson," said Jake, only 54 years old."

Further over, they found the Reverend Barclay's grave. He had died some 15 years after they had left the Victorian era. Beth found Gerald Black's family vault and from the inscription was very pleased to learn that he had married Martha, Simon's mother. Simon had been buried in the same grave, some thirty years later, but the other Black family members could not be found. Lisa probably married and would be under a different name, as would Gerald's own daughters.

Only one Mandeville grave was found and from the dates, they worked out it was Lewis' grandfather, who had lived another ten years, to the ripe old age of 92. They assumed the family must have moved on from Wattle Peak, after his death.

Rachel the cook and Jacob, her husband, were there and as they married late in life it was nice to see they managed a good many years together and Beth hoped they had been happy.

"In the spring I'll bring flowers for them all," said Beth, as she thought of each of them in turn and smiled. They finished standing by Great Uncle Sedgwick and Great Aunt Anna's graves which were alongside each other. "It's a pity we never knew her," she sighed.

The following week, Henry handed to his three excited children, Great Aunt Anna's journal and the letters. They hurried up to Beth's room, where she allowed the boys to laze on her bed, as she made herself comfortable in her old armchair. "Read the letter first," suggested Mike.

*Dear Albert and children*

*As promised, I take pen in hand to tell you how I have fared so far from Pennington.*

*I'm now, at long last, on the island of Jamaica with Giles. We spent two weeks in the capital, Kingston, where once more I got my land legs back. It was a very busy place and there I picked up supplies for my new school.*

*I saw many sailing ships in the harbour, stocking up with sugar and rum for their trips to England and Europe. I was surprised by the many nationalities working in the port.*

*We eventually re-boarded the same ship for the final leg of the journey, to a port and town called Martha Brae, in Montego Bay, in a county called Cornwall. There is little resemblance to the same county that you know back in England.*

*The island is very green and the jungle dense. It is almost impenetrable, with many strange trees where it hasn't been cleared. There are trees called 'palm trees' and one type, the coco, produces huge nuts. The inner shell has a sweet white flesh with a hollow centre contains a liquid similar to watery milk.*

*The majority of the populace are black with tight curly hair, their teeth seem very white against their dark skins. Some of these are freemen and it is those who are seen in the town. They are a cheerful and smiling people. The freemen, living where I am, have only rather ramshackle huts and like the poor everywhere, they are badly clothed. The rest, some 30.000, maybe more, are slaves and are kept on the plantations that grow the sugar cane, that has made so many people rich back in England. The warm seas here are full of many beautiful, colourful, fish that are very tasty to eat and the jungle contains large hairy spiders and yellow snakes, both of which can be poisonous, so you need to keep to the open trails. At harvest time the snakes hide in the cane fields and kill many slaves.*

*In Martha Brae, a few buildings similar to those at home, can be seen. The school house is new and made entirely of wood and it's painted a light blue. Nearby, there is a very large guest house, where some of the boys attending the school will be housed. The entire top floor is used just for them, as their families live too far away for them to travel home each day, to one of the many huge plantations. Mrs Watson and her daughter Matilda, who arrived here from Portsmouth a few years ago run the guest house.*

*I shall have a class of twenty in due course, made up from both the plantation owners' children and those of the overseers.*

*The sky here is a vivid blue and the sun so hot each day that I now have a wide brimmed hat made from the palm leaves. The leaves are useful in all sorts of ways, such as for making baskets, mats and even ropes.*

*I have seen the large areas cleared of jungle, where the sugar cane grows, acre after acre. The plants are as tall as a man and at the moment these are turning from green to yellow. It is dry now, but once the rainy season arrives in October, there will be torrential rain every afternoon, sometimes for hours at a time and it will be very humid and quite sticky, or so I have been warned.*

*The master of the ship that brought me here, has agreed to take back, to Hayle, a crate of coconuts for you all to share and a hat for your teacher. He will be in contact, soon after he arrives back.*

*Yours with affection*
*James Pendleton.* *1763 June.*

"I like the little drawings James did around the pages, a palm tree with a little black boy smiling, as he sits below it," said Beth.

"There's a coconut cut in half, showing the layers and what they are used for," added Mike.

"Look at the drawings of the school house and guest house and those strange looking fishes," commented Jake.

"The flowers are quite unusual," said Beth, handing the letter to the boys, to study.

"Well, at least we know he got to Jamaica safely," stated Mike.

"Yes, but I don't like the sound of those spiders," said Jake, with a shudder.

"Or the snakes," chipped in Beth, as she grimaced.

"Let me read the next letter," pleaded Mike. So Beth handed it over and settled back to listen.

*Dear Albert*

*Many thanks for your letter. I'm glad the school and its pupils are flourishing so well under your care.*

*The school here has also gone from strength to strength. I now have 30 pupils as some local tradesmen have enrolled their children.*

*Giles asked me to spend the Easter break at his plantation, some thirty miles from here. It was a wearisome journey as we went by mule. His plantation is very well run, unlike some. Giles has taken the trouble to see just how his workers are treated. He sacked one of the overseers, when he found he was too fond of using the lash. I'm not sure if it was out of compassion or just that he realised such punishment left the men unable to work for several days. I hope it was the former.*

*Giles and I had many heated discussions about the need for slavery on our journey here and he knows well my opposition to the practice. I was pleased to hear from him that he has seen to it that his slaves are well housed and well fed. As a result, his sugar production has improved so not a completely selfless act I fear. However, some good has come of it.*

*He will see that you get this letter, as he is to spend the next year or so in England and will return here in about 18 months, if he can persuade his wife to come back with him.*

*The rainy season was as bad as predicted. It left you clammy from the humidity, needing to change your clothes several times a day, as a result. In addition, you got drenched, if not indoors, when the rain started. The heat, at times, leaves you drained and very tired so lessons are cut short on the worst days or are started very early to make the most of the coolest part of the day. At least we don't suffer the cold harsh winters that you have so that is a blessing.*

*Mrs Watson put on a grand Christmas dinner for me and those pupils who stayed over the festive season. We had a turkey rather than a goose, a large less fatty bird, brought here from America. Matilda, helps me a great deal with the children, especially if they are unwell, mends their clothes and comforts the homesick ones. I'm very fond of her. She is very pretty, has dark brown hair, blue eyes and laughs a great deal.*

*I was so pleased that you got the coconuts and the hat. Give my regards to the children and my friends in Pennington.*

*Yours truly*

*James Pendleton. 30 December 1764.*

"What a nice letter, he had obviously settled in and was happy," said Beth. She picked up her great aunt's journal, a slim book and opened it carefully and read aloud:-

*'My quest started, when I as the local historian, found amongst the various records for Pennington, a box relating to its workhouse. To my amazement, at the bottom of the box, I found papers belonging to the Joseph House School and Home for Children. My heart nearly missed a beat. When I opened the letters addressed to the school I was elated when I saw James's handwriting once more as I read that he made it safely to Jamaica. I have wondered for many years what had happened to him. Now I'm on my way to the island.'*

*I lifted my face to absorb the May sunshine as I stood on the ship's deck, setting forth on my long awaited trip to Jamaica, with Portsmouth slipping gradually from my view. I felt a little sad, as Sedgwick has been unable to accompany me, as planned. His wife had been seriously ill, so he would not leave her.*

*I am excited; knowing that in two weeks I shall be in Jamaica, a fraction of the time it must have taken James to travel the distance. I'm travelling on the SS Trafalgar, a cargo ship, that also takes up to twenty passengers. My cabin is quite nice, if a little on the small side and I'm looking forward to the wonderful sunshine. Our own spring has been so cold until now.*

*It has been a quiet journey and the weather has been improving, day by day. Now, at the end of my first week, I have finally met all my fellow passengers. Some had suffered bouts of sea sickness, though I can honestly say the seas have been relatively calm. I spend most of my days with them, lazing around on deck, being waited upon.*

*Dr West and his wife sit with me at dinner each night, they are returning to Kingston, after a vacation in England. I was pleased when he told me, that with it being May, the rainfall should be light, so the roads, though in poor condition, would be passable unlike in the wet season.*

*I explained I had but two days in Kingston to seek advice regarding tracing James's footsteps. Thereupon, they offered to see me to my hotel and to point out the municipal buildings and the library. I shall continue, thereafter, with the ship to Martha Brae, on the north coast.*

*The ship docked early in the morning at the end of our second week. The harbour was extremely busy. I saw huge piles of sacks of sugar, hands of bananas and casks of rum as ships from all around the Caribbean, South America, the United States and, of course, Europe were being loaded up.*

*I set off with my suitcase, in a taxi along with the Wests. They pointed out key buildings on our route, before dropping me at the hotel, in the city centre. We agreed to meet again on my return from the north west of this large island, which is some 230km (145miles) long and 80 km (50 miles) wide.*

*That afternoon, I visited the registry of births, deaths and marriages. Miss Worth, a young black woman, came to my assistance. I explained about James from what details I had. I'd assumed he was born in 1739, as he was sixteen years of age when I last had a record of him in 1755.*

"Yes, that's the date we assumed he would have used," said Jake, "after all, he could not use 1893, his real year of birth." He saw Beth's look of slight impatience, "Sorry, Beth, please carry on."

*Miss Worth came back after a half hour search. She was sorry, but there was no trace of him. Not all of the records had been transferred to the main registry, especially the very early ones and, of course, when there had been hurricanes or earthquakes some records had been lost. She then told me not to give up hope. As he was a teacher, I should check with the library, as they have some records relating to the townships. So, a little despondent, I hurried out into the heat making my way back to the hotel, to my large room with its cooling ceiling fan. That day was particularly hot, as there was little or no wind.*

*The following morning, I entered the library and there, with help, found a record confirming that a new school had been set up in Martha Brae, in 1763. The first school master came from England, one James Pendleton, but he ceased to work there in 1770. The librarian explained that in that year Sir William Trelawney had become the Governor of Jamaica and had split the parish of St James into two. The one parish was named Trelawney, after him. It was then, that the village of Falmouth started to grow into a town and a proper port established.*

*This new township, with its government offices, was eventually to outshine Martha Brae, the previous capital of the county of Cornwall. Falmouth became the chief town, so it's likely he moved there, suggested the librarian. They would have been looking for people, such as teachers, because of its quickly growing population.*

*The ship left the following morning at 8am and I settled in for the trip around to the other side of the island. I had an overnight stay booked in at the local Inn, in Martha Brae. At 1pm, I was safely ashore. I left my suitcase at the Inn and anxiously set off to find the local library, where they had archives of the local newspaper, from 1770 onwards. After a few hours searching, I came across details of the wedding reception of a local teacher and his bride, held at the town's main guest house, next to the school. It was also a farewell party for the couple, Matilda Watson and her new husband, James Pendleton, as they were leaving for Falmouth.*

*I travelled to Falmouth by a small sailing boat the next day. There, I was pleasantly surprised to see how much of the old town remained, including the house owned by Elizabeth Barrett Browning the poetess, though she was never well enough to go there. It was her family that provided much of the land, used for the once extremely prosperous harbour.*

*Having found a room at a local hotel, I went in search and found the local historian, Mr Hard and explained my problem. He was able to check the school records. James became a master at Trelawney School in 1770 but ceased in 1775. While Mr Hard escorted me to St Christopher's Church, he explained that the year 1775 was a significant one in the town's history, as many had died of Yellow Jack fever. It was a type of malaria that attacks the liver, causing the victim's skin to appear yellow. The coastal areas were rarely infected, but the mosquito that carried the fever came in during a hurricane.*

*We searched for the two graves, but could find nothing and I sadly decided it was time to go back to my room and think again. We were about to leave, when Mr Hart moved over to a large wide gravestone covered with ivy and pulled this carefully away. There we stood and read together the inscription:*

'James Pendleton and his beloved wife Matilda.
Died 6th May 1775'

*'After tirelessly caring for their pupils and many others, during an outbreak of Yellow Jack fever -1st Feb 1775 – 7th May1775, they too succumbed to the fever.'*

*'Erected by the grateful parents of the pupils of Trelawney School.'*

*I stood, stunned and so proud. I had always known he was someone special. I had tears in my eyes, he was only 36 years old still a young man. I took out my camera and took pictures to show Sedgwick, on my return.*

*The following morning, I took a large bunch of local flowers to place on their grave. I spent a few days more exploring Falmouth. Many of the buildings had been preserved making it a historian's paradise. I visited the places that James would have known and walked the streets he would have walked and was pleased he had been happy once more, albeit for only a few years.*

Beth and her brothers were sad to read of James's end and looked at the photos Anna had pasted in the journal.

Anna ended her journal with details of her return to Kingston and the time she spent with the Wests, before her return to England and how she had bought and carefully packed, a wide brimmed hat for Sedgwick, made of palm leaves, knowing it would make him smile.

Beth turned over the remaining empty pages in the journal and found a note on the last page, stating the vicar thought he had seen another box of records relating to the orphanage, if she was interested. Beth wondered whether Great Aunt Anna had bothered to follow this up on her return from the West Indies, having already found, by then, her beloved James's Grave. "Let's visit the vicar again and see those school and orphanage records, I would like to know what else happened to the school and orphanage before the buildings ended up in the hands of the parish council.

The vicar was busy in his garden when the children called to see him. "Come in, please," he said.

"Thank you," said Mike, as they all entered the hall. The vicar ushered them into the sitting room, while he went to wash his hands. "So, what can I do for you today?" he remarked, as he entered the room.

"Well, said Beth, "we have been reading our Great Aunt Anna's journal, about her search for a James Pendleton, who went to live in the West Indies in the 1700's. There's a note about some later records you had found, relating to the school and orphanage, where James had worked in Pennington. We would like to follow up on their history and wondered if you might still have them?

"Oh, yes, your Great Aunt never came to collect them. She was so happy with concluding her investigation that she must have forgotten about them. I did read her journal, you know, and could see why she might not have needed them anymore."

"So, do you have them here?" asked Beth

"I believe I do. Why don't you make us all a cup of tea and I'll go check the attic; they are kicking around in there somewhere," He smiled, as the children headed for the kitchen as he made his way up the stairs. Beth heard the rattle of the attic ladder as it was pulled down. She found the tea tray and Mike got out the cups and saucers. Jake handed her the milk jug and sugar bowl, as the vicar called for Mike to come and help with the box.

Mike and the vicar entered the sitting room, managing to carry a small tea chest between them, as Beth placed the heavy tray on the coffee table and began to pour the tea. "There you are," said the vicar, as he released his grip on the box and sat down next to Beth. "You can take it home and read it all at your leisure. It might take you are while from the amount in there. Let me have it back when you've finished."

"That's great," said Jake, who picked out a couple of the bundles.

"What, no biscuits?" said the vicar and disappeared into the kitchen to return with a tin. Opening the tin and handing it around, he asked the children what they thought of their Aunt's journal. Some half hour later the trio set off, the boys carrying the chest between them.

As they sat on the floor of their attic, Beth handed out bundles of paper to the boys to look through, while she sorted the school registers in order. These books covered five years each. The first book was ten years after James had left Cornwall. The top of the page showed the teacher's name, Albert Brindle, for the year 1770. The name changed in Sept 1774 to that of Mistress Mary Gibson, when the new school year started.

"Oh," said Beth, "I wonder what happened to Albert, you know, the teacher James wrote to when he arrived in Jamaica? He seems to have left the school in 1775."

Mike lifted out a small unopened package addressed to Albert. "Someone had written across it 'current address unknown'," said Mike. "Here, have a look at the parcel, it's never been opened." Each looked at it in turn. It was done up in sealing wax and string.

"Well, it's never going to be delivered now," said Jake, shaking it. "Let's open it."

Beth found a pair of scissors and cut the string, inside was a letter and another wrapped parcel. "What does it say?" asked

Jake, as he watched his sister open out a thick, yellowing sheet of paper. Sitting back on her heels, Beth read aloud:-

*Dear Albert*

*I have asked my good friend, Giles Pendleton to bring this letter to you, if I should die, which seems very likely. We are in the middle of an epidemic of Yellow Jack fever. Many of the school children have died and my lovely wife, Matilda, has become infected. There is no way I will leave her.*

*I have a particular favour to ask of you. The small parcel enclosed I want you to leave in the attic of the old farmhouse at Wattle Peak. There is a gap behind the bracket that holds up one of the front windows. Would you say nothing about it to the owners and just slide it out of sight in the gap. It is for a special friend, who will find it in due course.*

*I hope you and the children of the school are doing well. Thank you.*

*Yours sincerely,*

*James Pendleton 4th May 1775*

"That was only a couple of days before he died." said Beth, with a sigh. "Of course, it was never opened, as Albert had gone, so it never reached the gap in our attic. Surely it was meant for us. Who else knew about the gap?"

"Let me see the smaller parcel again," said Jake, taking it from Beth. "The writing has faded, but it looks like it's addressed to Michael Roberts, no, no I think it could be Robertson! Mike, it's for you," said Jake, his mouth fell open. Mike's hand shook, as he took the little parcel from Jake and tore open the brown wrapping paper. A note in Jamie's handwriting fell out.

*Dear Mike*

*Having no children of my own, I could think of no one, other than you to whom that I would rather give my family ring. I have enclosed it, along with, a few sovereigns, so Beth and Jake may also have rings of their choosing. You impressed me that night the housekeepers threaten to shoot you, your brother and sister, back in 1760. The way you stood between them and that wicked woman took courage. It is, therefore, my reward to you for your bravery.*

*I have had a good life in Jamaica and was lucky enough to find another woman to love and share my life, Matilda, though Lucinda still holds a place in my heart.*

*Good luck for the future.*

*Yours Jamie*

"Let's see it," said Jake, as Mike took the ring from out of its wrapping and placed it on his finger. The initial 'P' stood out, as did the engraved little rose. “How are we going to explain the ring turning up again?” said Jake.

“I’m sure Beth will come up with something,” said Mike, with a grin.

They found, from the records, that the school and orphanage lasted a further thirty years, until the money, left by ‘Highwayman Joe’ and a large donation made by Giles on his final return from Jamaica, ran out. The council took over the buildings when funds ran dry and used it as a workhouse. The three children returned the box of papers to the vicar, a few weeks later.

Beth gave back to her father their Great Aunt’s journal. “I have to admit, I’m puzzled, as I have not found a James Pendleton on the family tree for the years mentioned in my Aunt’s journal.”

“Did you not say Great Aunt Anna married a second cousin, whose name was also Pendleton? Perhaps James was on his side of the family,” remarked Beth.

“Yes, you’re right, so he could be a more distant relative.”

“You know, Dad, I think I might like to be an historian,” said Beth.

“Do you now. Well, we will have to see about that. If your exam results are as good as before, it may be a possibility.” He turned to the boys, “I hope you helped Beth put away the Victorian clothes properly?”

"Of course we did." they chorused, grinning at him.

"Your mother and I have had an idea about the trunks and wondered if you would consider setting up an exhibition in the attic each year, just for a few days or so, if we were to borrow a few mannequins for you. The proceeds could go to a charity"

"That's a nice idea, an annual exhibition, why not? After all we wouldn't like the collections to be forgotten about," replied Beth.

"You might even like to include some items from the Edwardian era, as there is a partly filled trunk in the main attic and other bits and pieces up there. I think Great Uncle Sedgwick had started to make another collection," added their father.

"Wow," said Jake. His father looked surprise.

"I never thought you, Jake, were so enthusiastic about history." Beth gave Jake a warning look.

As they left the study, Jake speculated as to whether this other trunk would have the same time travel possibilities as the others. "Don't get too excited, Jake, I really wouldn't think it likely," said Mike, "after all, the collection isn't complete and no books have been left for us. Fair's fair, we've been very lucky to have had such a gift that allowed us to visit three eras."

"It could be fun, just putting together another collection ourselves and writing up our own stories to be read by someone one day," said Beth.

“Perhaps one day another three children will enjoy Great Uncle Sedgwick’s gift,” added Jake. Just then Sooty barked as if he agreed with them, making the children laugh, as they went outside to enjoy the warm sunshine at Wattle Peak.

The End

## **Other books by Beth E Browning**

Going to a Party

Colours of Murder

Tales to be Told of Murder, Mayhem and Mystery

Tales to be Told of Love, Life and Farewells

## **Children Stories**

Two Adventure Stories :-

A World a Way - Josh Moon and Meg (6 year olds to 13years)

The Adventures of Bobo and Jojo (for children 4 years to 8)

## **Great Uncle Sedgwick' Gift - Part 1 & 2**

**(for all ages from 8 years old)**